Praise for T. Kingfisher

"The comedy that goblins deserve! A spry, plucky book about a band of goblins who want what we all do: to slack off without getting executed or ingested. What's more relatable than that?"
John Wiswell, award-winning author of
Someone You Can Build a Nest In

"Such a pleasure to read."
The New York Times

"Kingfisher never fails to dazzle."
Peter S. Beagle, Hugo, Nebula, and Locus
Award-winning author of *The Last Unicorn*

"Refreshing . . . a true comfort read."
The Washington Post

"Kingfisher is a master."
Travis Baldree, *New York Times* bestselling
author of *Legends & Lattes*

"Absolutely delightful and full of charm and truth."
Naomi Novik, *New York Times* bestselling
author of *A Deadly Education* and *Uprooted*

"The natural and inevitable heir to the greats of her genre."
Seanan McGuire, *New York Times* bestselling
author of *Every Heart a Doorway*

"Immensely charming, unexpected, full of heart."
Katherine Arden, bestselling author
of *The Bear and the Nightingale*

"An absolute joy . . . Kingfisher is endlessly inventive."
KJ Charles, author of *The Secret Lives of Country Gentlemen*

"T. Kingfisher's delicate, bittersweet style of fantasy
is like nothing else on shelves at the moment."
Paste

"Tucking into a T. Kingfisher book feels like coming
home . . . familiar, spectacular, and utterly surprising."
Vulture

Also by T. Kingfisher
and available from Titan Books

The Twisted Ones
The Hollow Places
Nettle & Bone
A House With Good Bones
Thornhedge
A Sorceress Comes to Call
Snake-Eater

THE SWORN SOLDIER SERIES
What Moves the Dead
What Feasts at Night
What Stalks the Deep

THE CLOCKTAUR WAR DUOLOGY
Clockwork Boys

T. KINGFISHER

TITAN BOOKS

Nine Goblins
Hardback edition ISBN: 9781835416525
Broken Binding edition ISBN: 9781835418550
E-book edition ISBN: 9781835416549
Paperback edition ISBN: 9781835416532

Published by Titan Books
A division of Titan Publishing Group Ltd
144 Southwark Street, London SE1 0UP
www.titanbooks.com

First Titan Books edition: January 2026
10 9 8 7 6 5 4 3 2 1

This is a work of fiction. All of the characters, organizations, and events portrayed in this novel are either products of the author's imagination or are used fictitiously. Any resemblance to actual persons, living or dead (except for satirical purposes), is entirely coincidental.

© Ursula Vernon 2013

T. Kingfisher asserts the moral right to be identified as the author of this work.

No part of this publication may be reproduced, stored in a retrieval system, or transmitted, in any form or by any means without the prior written permission of the publisher, nor be otherwise circulated in any form of binding or cover other than that in which it is published and without a similar condition being imposed on the subsequent purchaser.

A CIP catalogue record for this title is available from the British Library.

EU RP (for authorities only)
eucomply OÜ, Pärnu mnt. 139b-14, 11317 Tallinn, Estonia
hello@eucompliancepartner.com, +3375690241

Designed and typeset in Stempel Schneidler Std by Richard Mason.

Printed and bound by CPI Group (UK) Ltd, Croydon, CR0 4YY.

*For Kevin,
who had to put up with this
story for a very long time.*

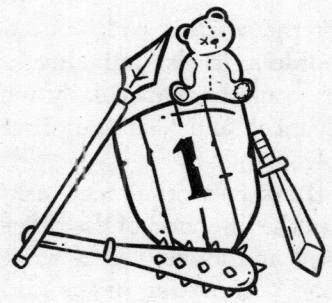

It was gruel again for breakfast.

It had been gruel for dinner the night before, and it would be gruel sandwiches for lunch, a dish only possible with goblin gruel, which was burnt solid and could be trusted not to ooze off the bread. It usually had unidentifiable lumps of something in it. Sometimes the lumps had legs.

Once, Corporal Algol had found an eyeball in his gruel, the memory of which he carried with him like a good luck charm and inflicted regularly on his fellow soldiers.

"Did I ever tell you guys about the time I found an eyeball—"

"Yes."

"Oh."

Algol wasn't a bad sort, really. He was bigger than usual for a goblin, a whopping four foot ten, with broad, knotty shoulders and enormous feet. He had the ocher-gray skin of a hill goblin, and he wasn't all that bright—but then, he was a goblin officer.

Smart goblins became mechanics. Dim goblins became soldiers. *Really* dim goblins became officers.

One of the latter was gesturing grandly from the top of a nearby rise. Nobody in the Nineteenth Infantry (better known as the Whinin' Niners) could hear what he was saying, but this was probably a good thing. If you couldn't hear what the officers said, you couldn't be said to be disobeying orders. It was amazing how selectively deaf goblin soldiers could be, particularly when words like "Charge!" and "Advance!" and "Get your finger out of there, soldier!" were involved.

"What do you think he's on about?" asked Weatherby, jerking his thumb in the direction of the officer.

Everybody turned and looked, since there was nothing else to do. They had been sitting in the middle of a stony wasteland for a week, and it was either watch the officers or watch the bird. (There was only the one bird, and it had been hanging around waiting for something to die for most of that week.)

The officer was waving his arms wildly now and hopping on one foot, like a man being attacked by ants. His red coat flapped in the breeze like shabby scarlet wings.

"We're going to move out," said Murray.

"You think?"

Murray nodded. "He's making a big speech. He only does that when he thinks we might get into a scrape with the enemy. The enemy's not gonna come at us here, so we must be moving out."

For a goblin, Murray was a genius. He'd washed out of the Mechanics Corps for being too good at his job. Goblins appreciate machines that are big and clunky and have lots of spiky bits sticking off them, and which break down and explode and take half the Corps with them. That's how you knew it worked. If it couldn't kill goblins, how could you trust it to kill the enemy?

Murray made small, neat, efficient devices that didn't even maim anybody during the construction phases. Nobody believed for a minute that the things would work, and Murray was sent down to the infantry in disgrace.

When his designs later proved dramatically successful, leaving enormous craters in the enemy ranks, and on one notable occasion, causing an entire platoon of elves to simultaneously wet themselves on the field of battle, nobody could remember who'd built them. There was such a rapid turnover in the Mechanics Corps that the people who'd thrown him out were now mostly scattered in bits across the landscape or had transferred back to Goblinhome to teach.

Murray was, therefore, the exception to the Whinin' Nineteenth—and indeed, to most of the surviving goblin infantry. "Too dim to desert. Too smart to die."

Even this was more clever than accurate. There are situations where no amount of smarts keeps you from getting killed. Blockhammer had been sitting down at breakfast a week ago, as canny a goblin veteran as you could wish for, and one of the supply rocs had gotten sweaty claws. The gigantic bird had been passing directly overhead, and the elephant it was carrying popped right out of its talons and landed directly on Blockhammer's head. (Also on his body, his camp stool, and all the space in a fifteen-foot radius around him.)

When they went to bury him, they couldn't figure out which bits were Blockhammer and which bits were the elephant, so the Nineteeth had buried his sword instead. They rolled a stone over it, and Murray wrote, "RIP-BLoKhaMer," on it (his genius did not extend to spelling), and Nessilka had sung a goblin lament. Everyone was very moved and toasted Blockhammer's memory repeatedly over the next batch of elephant gruel. (It was possible the gruel also contained bits of Blockhammer. Nobody wanted to dwell on this.)

The other half of the saying wasn't too accurate either. Weatherby, for example, had deserted no less than fifteen times, and he was so dim it was remarkable he hadn't been tapped as officer material.

It was really pretty easy to desert—people did it all the time—but Weatherby had made an art of it. He would nod to the rest of the Nineteenth, as they sat around the campfire, and say "Right, I'm off then!" and then walk in a straight line until he hit the edge of the Goblin Army encampment. Once he was fifty feet from the edge of camp, Weatherby proceeded to rip off his clothes, run to the nearest hill, rise, or tree stump, and begin dancing wildly in the moonlight, while shouting, "I'm free, you sods, free! I'm a free goblin! Waahoooo! *Free!*"

Eventually the guards would come get him and bring him home again, although his clothes were usually a loss.

Since the Goblin Army had blown almost all its uniform budget on red coats for the officers, everybody was wearing loincloths from home anyway, so nobody much noticed.

A runner came up to the edge of the fire where the Nineteenth were sitting. "New orders, Sergeant!" he said, saluting Nessilka.

Nessilka muttered something under her breath. She was the ranking member of the Nineteenth since Blockhammer had gotten splattered, followed by Murray and Algol, who were corporals, and everybody else, who weren't. You could tell the ranks by the stripes on the loincloth, although this system had drawbacks if you were trying to tell the difference between a general and somebody who just didn't do laundry often enough.

Nessilka didn't like being in charge. She was *good* at it, but she didn't like it. She had been the oldest of six children and was the veteran of three campaigns, and as a result, both responsibility and suspicion of rank were etched in Nessilka's bones. Finding herself as the senior member of the Whinin' Niners was like a constant itch between her shoulder blades.

"What's the word, then?" she asked.

"General Globberlich says to break camp. We're movin' out!" He saluted again. He had to be new. Nobody was that enthusiastic after the first month.

"Will do," said Nessilka, and waited.

The runner saluted again. He was a scrawny little

green fellow, probably with imp blood somewhere a few generations back.

He saluted for the fourth time, hard enough to bruise his forehead.

Sergeant Nessilka took pity on him and saluted back, and he ran off to the next camp.

Nessilka was a female goblin, which meant that everybody was a little scared of her. Occasionally you saw women in the enemy armies—generally slim, willowy young women with longbows and grim expressions. She wondered if everybody on their side tiptoed around them like naughty children with an unpredictable schoolteacher.

Somehow, she doubted it.

There was nothing slim or willowy about Nessilka. She was built like a chunk of granite, and she could carry a live boar under one arm. The only concession to femininity was that she wore her hair in a bun instead of a long queue, and she wore slightly fewer earrings than everyone else.

"All right, maggots, you heard the man," she growled. "Pack up and move out!"

Most of the Whinin' Nineteenth groaned and grumbled and sulked. Murray and Algol, however, got to their feet and went to start packing their kits, and eventually, the rest followed.

Sergeant Nessilka had just shoved her spiked club into her belt when a flash of red indicated that the officer had returned to his position on the cliff. Now he was mounted on his parade pig, a big white porker with its hooves polished and ribbons twined in its tail. He made a sweeping gesture with his sword. The pig squealed.

"And that's our cue," Nessilka said. She slung her pack over her shoulder and looked around her unit. They were mostly packed. Murray was helping the two newest recruits get their gear arranged. Algol had the lead rope for the supply goat. Gloober had a finger up his nose.

"Mooooooove OUT!"

The Whinin' Niners moved out.

How the Goblin War (if you asked the humans) or the Glorious Conflict Resisting The Ongoing Human Aggression (if you asked the goblin generals) or the Bloody Miserable Mess (if you asked the Nineteenth Infantry) got started really depends on which side was doing the talking.

Humans and elves will tell you that goblins are stinking, slinking, filthy, sheep-stealing, cattle-rustling, henhouse-raiding, disgusting, smelly, obnoxious, rude, unmannerly, and violent.

The goblins would actually agree with all that, and they might add "cowardly" and "lazy" to the list as well. Goblins have lots of flaws, but few illusions.

As far as the human side of the war is concerned, one day the goblins, who had been keeping to themselves pretty well in the high hills and deep mires, came out to a human settlement, riding their pigs and waving banners, and holding a list of really laughable demands.

The humans refused, and the next day they were hip-deep in short green-and-ocher people with tusks. The humans retaliated, the goblins retaliated for the retaliation, the elves got involved, the orcs got involved because the elves were involved, and by the end of six months it was a horrible, churning, entrenched mess, where troops on both sides sat around for weeks on end and occasionally ran at each other screaming.

Again, the goblins would agree with most of that account, but there was more to it than that.

Once upon a time, goblins had lived everywhere. Like rabbits, goblins are an immensely adaptable, quick-breeding lot, capable of living under practically any conditions. There are hill goblins and marsh goblins, forest goblins, who live in trees, and savannah goblins, who live in networked tunnels like prairie dog towns. There are desert goblins and jungle goblins, miniature island goblins and heavy-bodied tundra goblins. Goblins live *everywhere*.

Wherever a goblin happens to live, he complains about it constantly. This is actually a sign of affection. A desert goblin will complain endlessly about the beastly heat and the dreadful dryness and the spiky cactus. He will show you how his sunburn is peeling and the place where the rattlesnake bit him and the place where he bit the rattlesnake. He will be thoroughly, cheerfully, miserable.

If you took him away from the desert, he would be lost. He wouldn't know what to complain about. He might make a few half-hearted attempts, but he would eventually lapse into confused silence and return as quickly as possible to the desert he loves. Complaining is how he shows he's paying attention to all the little nuances of his home.

This is basically goblin psychology in a nutshell. Goblin cooks wait in anticipation for the rude comments about the flavor. A goblin courting the lady goblin of his dreams will point out the new lumps and splotches on her skin and ask if she's been sick lately because she looks off-color, and hey, is that a tick behind her left ear?

Goblins are in many ways stoics. When they're genuinely unhappy, they shut up and put their heads down and just try to blunder through. (Goblin divorces are notable for their lack of screaming.) If a goblin eats something without complaining, it was so bad he doesn't want to dwell on it. (Gruel among the Nineteenth Infantry had recently reached this point, and breakfast had become a silent, glum affair.)

A goblin trying to make the best of things is a very tragic sight indeed.

So the goblins lived over much of the land, and the woods and plains and deserts and whatnot rang with the cheery sounds of goblin complaints.

Then the humans came.

They came in small groups at first and cleared little clearings and built little houses, and the goblins didn't really mind. They're cowards, after all, and there was plenty of room, so they had no desire to forcibly evict the humans. They just avoided those places.

The clearings got bigger, and the houses got bigger, and the goblins kept avoiding them, until one day, there was hardly any place left that you weren't avoiding. And one by one, tribe by tribe, the goblins would melt quietly away into the wilderness, to impose on the hospitality of the next tribe over.

Sometimes, of course, it wasn't that easy. In a few cases, goblins wound up living on mountaintops and tunneling down instead of running away. On islands, they would have to steal boats and rafts from the humans and strike out across the ocean. Occasionally they couldn't find another island without people on it, and a whole colony of raft goblins sprang up, traveling with the currents, living on fish and seabirds and whatever they could steal from human settlements.

A knot of goblins even got stuck in a park for years, every avenue of escape having been filled in by a reasonably large city. They survived by panhandling and occasional muggings, and a fair number established themselves successfully in the sewers, where they breed riding rats the size of ponies and wrestle white alligators in the dark.

By and large, though, the goblins went deeper and deeper into the wilderness, and the wilderness got smaller and smaller and tamer and tamer. And then one day, a goblin scouting for new territory found himself standing on a beach, gazing out across the western sea.

It was the end of the road. They'd been pushed right to the edge of the continent, and there was simply no place else for them to go.

Sings-to-Trees had hair the color of sunlight and ashes, delicately pointed ears, and eyes the translucent green of new leaves. His shirt was off, he had the sort of tanned muscle acquired from years of healthy outdoor living, and you could have sharpened a sword on his cheekbones.

He was saved from being a young maiden's fantasy—unless she was a very peculiar young maiden—by the fact that he was buried up to the shoulder in the unpleasant end of a heavily pregnant unicorn. Bits of unicorn dung, not noticeably more ethereal than horse dung, were sliding down his arm, and every time the mare had a contraction, he lost feeling in his hand.

It had been nearly two hours, the ground was hard and cold, and his knees felt like live coals wrapped in ice. She'd kicked him twice, and if Sings-to-Trees hadn't known that it was impossible, he'd have begun to suspect that the unicorn had arranged a breech birth out of spite.

No, he was being unfair. It couldn't be any more fun for her than it was for him. Just because he didn't really like unicorns, he shouldn't let it cloud his judgment.

He sighed and tried yet again to get a grip on one of the foal's legs. Unicorn foals had hooves as delicate as glass bells, naturally, and however adorable they were when tripping lightly 'cross the meadow, they were pure torture to grab in the slippery, less-than-hospitable environment inside the mother unicorn.

If he could just get the little monster turned, a few good pushes should do it. The problem was getting a good grip. He rode out another contraction with gritted teeth.

Sings-to-Trees loved all living creatures with a broad, impartial love, the sort of love that rescues baby bats and stays up nights feeding them, one drop of milk and mealworm mix at a time. He splinted the legs of injured deer and treated mites in the ears of foxes and gave charcoal to colicky wyverns. No beast was too ugly, too monstrous, too troublesome. He had once donned smoked-glass goggles and shoulder-length cowhide gloves to sit up with an eggbound cockatrice for three days, giving it calcium tablets and oiling its cloacal vents every four hours. Since he'd been nursing a pocketful of baby hummingbirds at the time, which had to be fed sugar water every fifteen minutes sixteen hours out of the day, it had been quite an extraordinary three days. He still had nightmares about it.

But he'd never really warmed to unicorns. Possibly it was because they didn't need him. Regular elves loved unicorns, as they loved all beautiful creatures, and a unicorn with so much as a stubbed hoof could turn up at the door of any elf in the world and be assured of royal treatment. Sings-to-Trees hardly ever had to deal with them, and he preferred it that way.

But when somebody needed to actually reach a hand in there and turn a foal around, suddenly the unicorn lovers of the world melted away, and it was down to Sings-to-Trees and a barn and a bucket of soapy water. And the hind end of the unicorn, of course.

As if to punctuate this thought, the unicorn kicked him again. He grunted. He was pretty sure the mare was smart enough to know that he was helping her. He just didn't think she cared.

He got a grip on something that felt like a wee little

hock and started the tricky process of hauling, coaxing, and generally begging the tiny creature to turn around. Another contraction came along, and he willed his numb fingers to hold on to the foal's leg. His fingers laughed at him.

Give him trolls any day. A thousand pounds of muscle and bone, froggish, goatish creatures the size of grizzly bears, with enormous curling horns that could smash through a concrete wall. They were *ideal* patients. Trolls might not be any more talkative than unicorns, but they understood every word you said, and if they had come to you for help, they'd trust you to the ends of the earth. You could saw off a troll's leg, and it would look at you with huge, tearful eyes the size of dinner plates and hold still while you did it. And if you told them to come back in a week for a checkup, they'd be there a week later, as soon as the sun went down, squatting patiently in the vegetable patch, ready to be poked and prodded all over again. Sings-to-Trees quite liked trolls.

And they were *grateful*, too—not a month went by when he didn't wake up to see gigantic cloven hoofprints around the yard, and half a billy goat left draped across a tree stump.

Not like unicorns. As soon as the foal was able to walk, the mare would be gone like a shot, and he'd never see her again.

Come to think of it, maybe that wasn't a bad thing.

"Okay," he said to the unicorn, mildly surprised at the weariness in his own voice, "I think I've got it presenting right. Let's give this a try . . . PUSH!"

The mare pushed. He pulled. There was a brief horrible moment where nothing happened, and Sings-to-Trees saw another two hours of internal fumbling ahead of him, and then with almost absurd ease, the foal slid out and hit him in the chest, the mare grunted in triumph, and he fell over backward with his arms full of slimy baby unicorn.

Its first act was to kick him with its adorable little hooves. He gazed at the barn rafters while it beat a tattoo on his ribs. It hurt, but not as much as his knees did.

Okay. Not much more to go. He could handle this.

He staggered upright, shuffled on his knees to the end of the unicorn he hadn't seen much of this evening, and dumped the foal in front of her.

She bent down, snuffled at the tiny creature, tapped it delicately with her foot-long horn as if to test it, and then began licking at its damp white hide. The bedraggled foal lifted its muzzle and made a faint squeaky snort of protest.

Even to someone who didn't much care for unicorns, at another time, this scene would be pure magic, a reaffirmation of everything good and noble in the world. But there was gunk from the hind end of a unicorn plastered clear up the side of his face, delicate hoofprints were turning purple across his ribcage, and he felt about a thousand years old.

He got painfully to his feet—his knees had moved through the on-fire stage and now felt as if tiny wolverines were chewing under the kneecaps—and staggered outside to the pump. He tried to grab the pump handle, and for an awful minute his hand wouldn't close on it.

Well, no surprise there. His right arm, which had been the one inside the unicorn, was red and white and bruising magnificently where contractions had smacked his bicep repeatedly against the mare's pelvic bones, and there was unicorn crap and amniotic fluid and bits of straw all over him.

Sings-to-Trees slumped against the pump handle, moaned, and managed to grab it with his left hand. By dropping most of his weight on it, with all the grace of a sack of potatoes, he got enough water out to sluice the worst of the muck from him. It was icy cold, but he didn't really care.

There was soap somewhere. He found it. It didn't lather very well, but he made at least a symbolic effort before giving up.

He ducked his head back in the barn and glanced over at the mother and child, who were arranged in a beautifully domestic scene, as tranquil as the dawn. White hide glowed in the muted lamplight of the barn. You'd never know she'd spent hours in labor. That was unicorns for you.

Pausing only to make sure that the afterbirth had passed with no difficulties—he considered patting the foal, but the mare, ingrate that she was, stamped a hoof at him and lowered her horn warningly—Sings-to-Trees limped out of the barn.

The moon glared down like a bar of soap in a bucket of cold sky. The path up to the house was packed earth, washed blue and black in the moonlight, and approximately a thousand miles long. Several ages of the earth passed while he toiled up to the house, punctuated by the bright jangle of pain from his knees.

A coyote with one eye and a ragged ear was stretched out across the porch rug. When the elf was close enough, the coyote lifted his head, pricked up his good ear, and came down to meet Sings-to-Trees. A cold nose touched his hand, and the tail made a careless motion that was certainly not a wag—Fleabane had a certain amount of dignity, despite his name—but might conceivably be mistaken for one. Sings-to-Trees wound a cold hand in the coarse hair behind the coyote's ears and rubbed affectionately. They walked the last few yards up to the house together, and then Fleabane flopped back down on the rug, and Sings-to-Trees went inside.

There were animals to be fed yet—a bat hanging upside down in the closet who was thankfully past needing ground mealworms shoved down its throat, an orphaned raccoon who was just starting on solid foods and needed warm milk with a little bread, and of course the gargoyle. He dumped a handful of dried mealworms on the closet floor, heard a grumpy chitter in response, and left the bat to its own devices.

There was cold chicken left, and he divided it up carefully, a quarter for a sandwich, and three quarters for the gargoyle. He built up the fire and set milk to warm by the hearth. The warmth was wonderful, if painful on his cold hands. He started to sink down into the rug in front of the fireplace, caught himself, and lurched to his feet. He didn't dare stop moving. If he sat down to rest, he wasn't going to get back up in a hurry.

The back door opened with a wooden groan. He took three steps forward, turned, and hucked the battered remains of the chicken onto the roof.

A stony chuckling came down to him, followed by the crunch of chicken bones. Satisfied, Sings-to-Trees went back inside to feed the raccoon.

He must have made tea at some point because when he woke up, there was a stone-cold mug of it next to his elbow and a half-eaten sandwich sliding off his knee. The raccoon cub was asleep on his lap, in the wreckage of what had been a saucer full of bread soaked in warm milk. Perhaps it was just as well he hadn't bothered with a shirt.

It looked like most of the milk had gone into the raccoon, anyway, and his sandwich had a distinctly gnawed look. Some days, that was all you could ask for.

Sings-to-Trees gave up even pretending he was awake. He put the raccoon to bed, toweled off the remnants of both their dinners as best he could, and limped to the bedroom. He had just enough energy to remove his shoes, and then sleep crept up and hit him.

The Nineteenth Infantry were marching, if you could call it that.

Goblins march badly. They have enormous thick feet like elephants, so they are quite good at walking, but they have no rhythm, and very few goblins have ever mastered the ability to tell left from right without stopping to think about it. So when somebody yells, "Left foot, right foot!" there is generally a long silence while the goblins all try to remember which is which.

At some point, one bold goblin will step out, and all the others follow immediately in the hope he knows what he's doing. It's about a fifty-fifty shot if he's leading with the correct foot or not, but at least they're all wrong together.

On a good day, they will stay in step for nearly a minute before somebody gets bored, or trips, or stumbles, or forgets what he's doing and begins skipping. Small knots break off. Officers ride around on their pigs, shouting orders and leaving havoc in their wake.

Eventually the better sergeants round up their units and herd them more or less in the direction that everybody seems to be going. In fits and starts, the Goblin Army lurches on.

Nessilka was a fairly good sergeant and had most of the Whinin' Niners aimed in the correct direction. Algol and the pack mule formed the nucleus of the group, and since he was taller than most of the other goblins, everybody was able to keep him in sight.

At the moment, Nessilka's greater concern was the two new recruits.

They were identical twins, which gave her a headache, and they were young and bright-eyed and enthusiastic and finished each other's sentences, which took the headache to a whole new level.

"Where are we . . ."

". . . going, Sarge?"

"We don't know. We just follow orders and go there."

They gave her identical nods.

"Will we be . . ."

". . . fighting, Sarge?"

"Sooner or later, yes."

Everyone stumped along in silence for a while. The flat stony badlands were giving way to little lumpy hills and the occasional scrubby tree, with more trees on the horizon. The wind that came to them smelled like pine, which was a big improvement over goblin.

The new recruits had the standard loincloth from home, made out of the standard rancid goat hide, and they both had what passed for weaponry in the Goblin Army—a board with a nail in it. Unless she managed to beat some kind of sense into them, Nessilka gave them a week.

"So you're twins," she said, by way of an opening gambit.

"Yes, Sarge!" they said in unison.

"How should I tell you apart?"

"You . . ."

". . . don't."

"Not even our mom . . ."

". . . can tell us apart."

"We'll fix that," she said grimly, and beckoned to Thumper.

Thumper would need thick-soled boots to stand four feet tall, but he was at least four feet wide. His biceps were the size of badgers, and he had no neck. He did not use a shield, preferring to carry two large spiked maces, both taken from the fallen foe. When he was hitting things, there was a joyful gleam in his eye, and when he wasn't, there was a glitter that indicated he was probably *thinking* about hitting things.

He had no personality that Nessilka had ever been able to uncover—possibly it had gone off with his neck somewhere—but he was an excellent goblin to have at your side in a fight.

"Recruits, this is Thumper."

"Hi, Thumper!" chorused the twins.

Thumper treated this the way he treated everything that did not involve hitting things—he eyed it warily to see if there was any potential hitting to be had, and then ignored it.

"Thumper," she said, "I can't tell these two apart."

Thumper nodded.

"Fix that," she said.

He nodded again, turned around, and punched the one on the left in the face.

The recruit fell over. The other recruit gaped at him.

Thumper picked the damaged recruit up, nodded to the sergeant, and wandered off.

The unfortunate goblin swayed on his feet. His left eye was already swelling and would shortly be turning a striking shade of purple.

"That's better," said Nessilka. "Now, then. The first thing you should learn is to *never* tell a superior officer what they can't do."

They looked at her with identical miserable expressions (except for the swollen eye). "We're sorry, Sarge."

"Yeah, well . . ." Nessilka squelched a nagging feeling of guilt. It was a hard world and a hard war, and the sooner they learned it, the better. "What are your names?"

"Mishkin," said the one on the right.

"Mushkin," said the one with the swollen eye.

"Right. The next thing you should learn is how to take a

punch a little better than that, but it'll have to wait until we stop for the night. Have you had any training at all?"

"We had two weeks..."

"...of boot camp, Sarge."

The sergeant grunted. "Whacked a lot of straw men with your board, eh?"

Mishkin nodded vigorously. Mushkin nodded rather more gingerly, holding his face.

Up ahead, Weatherby was drifting off to the side. Nessilka could tell he was planning to make a break for it, because he was starting to mutter to himself and tug at his clothes. She sighed and did what sergeants have done since time immemorial... she delegated.

"Go see Corporal Algol and tell him that you've had the basic boot camp and nothing else. And that I said to put something on that eye."

"Yes, Sarge!"

The twins went to find Algol, and Nessilka went to collar Weatherby.

SINGS-TO-TREES'S MORNING BEGAN slightly after dawn, when the hen crowed.

She was a black hen with a fine gold eye and a blue sheen to her feathers. She laid quite large brown eggs. She also mounted the other hens occasionally, an exercise in bafflement for everyone involved. And every morning, she crowed.

As far as he could tell, she seemed happy, so he'd resigned himself to getting up at hen's-crow most mornings. He hadn't wanted a rooster, anyway. His farm was located on the edge of what were nominally the Elvenlands. A small human settlement lay less than an hour's walk away, where woods gave way to farmland. The humans viewed him as falling somewhere between the priest and the village idiot, and thus requiring feeding either way. Depending on the time of year, gifts of flour or cheese or bacon were always turning up, and they dumped excess chicks on him year-round. He had a hard enough time keeping up with donated chickens—had his small flock been producing more on their own, he'd have been hip-deep in fowl. So he was really rather grateful for the hen, after all.

This morning, there was a small, fresh cheese on the doorstep, accompanied by a small jug of buttermilk. He took both inside. Fleabane was gone, on some coyote-ish errand of his own, or there would have been toothmarks in the cheese.

Elf and raccoon shared a pleasant breakfast. It was a little over a month old—the raccoon, not the breakfast—with big, wide eyes and delicate, dexterous black fingers, and it was shortly going to be tearing his house apart. The destructive capacity of small cute animals was really quite astonishing. Fortunately, after years of this sort of thing, Sings no longer had much that could be torn apart. His furniture was heavy wood, scarred by claws and chewed by tiny (and occasionally not so tiny) teeth, the cushions faded by hundreds of washings, the rugs ragged and warm and mostly colorless.

He owned quite a few rugs. He had to wash them so often that it made sense to keep extras. An elven visitor had once commented (with the air of one desperately trying to find something complimentary to say) about the unusual patterns dyed into the rug. Sings-to-Trees had to explain that it wasn't dyed, precisely, but marked by numerous Mystery Stains from patients who had not been entirely in control of their bladders. The silence had been awkward.

He suspected the other elf had been expecting something on the order of a hermit monk, communing with nature and binding up the wings of snow-white doves with snow-white bandages, not a bedraggled lunatic daubed with unspeakable substances, surrounded by shrieking birds, and massaging the belly of a tiny lynx kitten to make it defecate. (In Sings-to-Trees's defense, it had been a particularly maddening week, with two lynx kittens, a nestful of orphaned gray jays, an infant false-phoenix that kept exploding into flames when startled, and a pine marten with a broken foot, who would have happily eaten any of the other patients if he could have caught them.) The other elf hadn't been back.

The raccoon trundled away from its food, stood up briefly on its hind legs, wobbled, and tried to steady itself against his mug. The mug went over. The raccoon also went over. He could only catch one, and of course, there was no question.

The raccoon snuggled against his chest and went "Clur-r-r-p!" The mug went "plunk!" The buttermilk went into his lap.

"Bad raccoon."

"Clurr-up!"

Well, it was his own fault for trying to feed himself and the creatures at the same time. The raccoon cub went back into its hutch by the hearth. He toweled off the worst of the buttermilk, and then the remains of the raccoon's breakfast. The mug had survived intact.

Had he been inclined to collect blown glass sculptures, he would have lived a life of great frustration, but his tastes had been limited by necessity to things that could take a heavy pounding. The mug, for example, was attractively glazed earthenware—pretty enough, but durable, and easily replaced if, say, a raccoon got into a cupboard, had the door swing shut behind it, and tried to smash its way out.

Unfortunately, this meant that there was very little elven about his home, as durability went somewhat against the prevailing elven aesthetic of things brought briefly from the earth, and then given back. A litter of fox cubs could give things back to the earth at an extraordinary rate, generally before the owner was quite done with them. Sings resigned himself to art made by humans and occasionally dwarves. As sacrifices went, he'd made worse.

Speaking of sacrifices . . .

He dumped the mug in the washbasin, shoved his feet into boots, squared his shoulders, and went to see if the unicorn was still there.

"Two weeks of boot camp, eh?" said Algol. He was digging in the pack goat's packs until he came up with a dubious bit of steak left over from the elephant (or possibly Blockhammer). "Here, put this on your eye."

The steak was cold, thanks to Murray. He had invented a device that kept meat cold, a small box with a fan and little metal wings. He claimed the wings dispersed heat. Most of the other goblins thought he was loony, but Algol had made an effort to understand. "Like birds!" he'd said.

Murray had stared at him, wiping sweat from under his goggles.

"Hot air rises," Algol tried to explain, "so birds must be hot because they fly. The wings cool them down so they can land without floating away."

"Riiiiight," Murray had said. "Ah . . . yeah. Just like that. How . . . *novel* of you to figure that out."

Algol was proud.

Mushkin put the steak on his eye. Mishkin hovered nervously. "Will he be okay? Should he go to the medics?"

"You in a big hurry to lose the eye?" asked Algol mildly. "Keep the steak on it, you'll be fine." He had figured out that the best way to deal with the twins was to address them as one goblin with four arms and two heads.

"This is Buttercup." Algol nodded to the supply goat.

"Hi, Buttercup!" the twins chorused.

Up ahead, Sergeant Nessilka cringed. Why had she let him name the goat? You shouldn't name the goat. It was just "the goat." If food got scarce enough, you ate the goat, and that was much harder when it had a name.

Algol was a good goblin, and a fairly reliable corporal, but he had some odd blind spots, often where animals were involved.

"Now then. Boot camp. Kill a lot of straw men?"

"Yes, Algol!"

"S'fine if we're fighting scarecrows, I s'pose. Unfortunately, we're fighting elves. You ever *seen* an elf?"

"No . . ."

"We heard they were eight feet tall and breathed fire from their nostrils!" said Mushkin from under his steak.

"Generally not, no."

The average elf, the corporal explained, was a little under six feet tall, with pasty skin like a mushroom and long, pointy ears like a mule. "They're fast, see? Not goblin fast, but quick as weasels. And they have really good weapons. Loot their weapons if you get a chance." He patted the sword at his side. It had runes like wriggling worms all down the length, which Murray said meant "Blade that Dances in the Houses of the Moon" in Elven.

Algol called it "Bob," after his goldfish back home.

"If you loot their packs, they've usually got decent vittles, too. Vegetarian, but it's good in stew. Their armor doesn't fit us for beans, so don't bother."

Mishkin and Mushkin listened with round eyes, absorbing it all.

"Now, if we get in a fight—err—"

He looked at the twins. They looked back guilelessly. Algol sighed.

"If we get in a fight, try to stay close to me."

He wracked his brain.

"They're all a lot taller than we are, so go for the legs.

Hardly anybody has any armor on the back of their knees. We'll try to find you a shield. Hold the shield over your head, and go for the knees."

"Always go for the knees..."

ALWAYS GO FOR *the knees* was, in fact, the family motto of Clan Uggersplut, to which Algol belonged in a roundabout fashion involving several second cousins and a yak.

Uggersplut, as it happened, was also the clan to which the most competent of the ranking generals of the Goblin Army also belonged.

It had been the scions of Uggersplut who carried the demands of the goblins to the humans, long ago, at the start of the war.

Goblins, much like rats, prefer to flee, but when they're cornered . . . well. When the goblin scout had arrived on the shore of the western sea, the goblin tribes had turned, all together, like an enormous green rat at bay, and bared their collective teeth.

So the goblin leaders sat down, in the mountain called Goblinhome—half city, half refugee camp—and talked for three days and two nights. As the sun set on the third day, they signed the large warthog hide on which their demands were written. Then they drew straws for who would carry it to the humans.

Clan Uggersplut had drawn the short straw.

Mounted on their best steeds, their faces marked with elaborate tribal patterns in black earth, coup markers braided into their hair, Uggersplut rode down from the mountains to the largest of the nearby human settlements. Single file, heads held high, they rode through the center of the town, and stopped in the central square, and demanded to see the leader of the town.

Many of the subtleties were lost on the humans. The lean

bodies of war-pigs in fighting trim looked feral and half-starved to human eyes, and the patterns of black earth, in which a goblin could have read whole volumes about tribal affiliations and clan standing, looked like streaky dirt and caked dust. Coup markers of bone and stone, denoting enemies slain and great deeds done, were seen as garbage trapped in unwashed hair. Where goblins would see high-ranked emissaries in full regalia, the humans saw a raggle-taggle band, ill-kempt and filthy, to be held in pity and contempt.

The mayor came out to meet them. To give what little credit he was due, he probably thought he was trying to be kind.

"Goblins, huh? You, um, want beer?" he asked, hunkering down in front of Severspine, the heir to Clan Uggersplut. "We, um, give you beer, you go away."

"We have come to discuss the ongoing human expansion," said Severspine coldly. "We want our lands back."

"*Good* beer," said the mayor, winking at the townspeople over Severspine's head.

Negotiations did not proceed well after that.

Three days later, the war had started, and nothing much would ever be the same again.

THEY'D BEEN MARCHING half the night. A halt had been called for fifteen minutes, which was time enough for Murray to whip out his small travel stove and make tea. The Nineteenth crowded around, brandishing their tin mugs and watching with owlish intensity.

Goblin tea resembles a nice cup of Earl Grey in much the same way that a catfish resembles the common tabby. They share a name, but one is a nice thing to curl up with on a rainy afternoon, and the other is found in the muck at the bottom of polluted rivers and has bits of debris sticking to it.

Murray poured the tea. Hands went into packs and came

out with fistfuls of crude rock sugar. The resulting brew resembled a kind of sweet gritty mud. Sounds of slurping were followed immediately by cheerful complaints.

"Tastes like rat squeezins."

"Huh, we haven't had anything as good as rat squeezins for six months. Tastes like a water buffalo got sick."

"I'd *kill* for some good rat squeezins."

Thus complimented, Murray beamed.

A pig-rider cantered down the road and pulled up in a squealing cloud of dust in the center of the Whinin' Niners. Nessilka saluted in a desultory fashion. Pig-riders were generally a higher class of messenger idiot than runners, but still nothing to get excited about.

"What's the word, then?" she asked.

"Another hour, then we're in position and make camp. Dawn attack, so sleep fast."

"Dawn? We'll get, like"—she did a little mental math—"four hours of sleep! After a day's march!"

The messenger grimaced. His pig danced under him. "General's orders."

"Yeah, not your fault." Nessilka waved him on. "Thanks."

It always takes longer to get somewhere than you think it will, and this is twice as true in the military, so the goblins marched into camp a mere three hours before dawn.

"Okay, troops, equipment check, and then get some sleep. We're getting up too damn early, so catch what you can."

The tents went up quickly. When your tent is three sticks and a whole cowhide, there's not a lot of time spent dithering. At the beginning of the campaign, the cowhides had been uncured, with the resulting smell of rotting leather and ripe goblin, but Murray had gotten the bright idea to salt the things. The end result was a kind of tent jerky. It still didn't smell great, but it kept the rain off, even if folding the hides was becoming increasingly problematic.

Nessilka figured if worse came to worst, they could always eat the tents.

"Is it even worth . . ."

". . . going to sleep?" asked the twins.

"Boys, it's always worth going to sleep. Sleep whenever you get the chance, because you don't know how long it's going to be until the next time."

"And eat," said Algol from behind her.

"Thank you, yes, Corporal. If there's food available, eat it. Meals can get awfully thin on the ground sometimes."

She glanced around the group to see who looked the least tired. "Gladblack, you're on second watch. I'll take first." Since there were plenty of sentries around the edge of the army, there wasn't much point in watching for the enemy, but you never knew when one of the other units was going to sneak over and try to nick your goat.

A teddy bear popped into her field of view. Nessilka winced, but it was only Blanchett.

"He wants to know when we're attacking," said the owner of the teddy bear.

"Tell him dawn," said the sergeant.

Blanchett, unlike much of the Nineteenth, wore a helmet. It was a complicated mass of fangy bone and spiky metal. He had taken it from a dead orc, and it didn't fit terribly well, but Blanchett almost never took it off, even to sleep.

You couldn't really blame him. A few months back, the Mechanics Corps had been working on a design for a new showerhead. The resulting explosions had involved terrific loss of life on both sides, and Blanchett had taken a flying log upside the head.

A battle had been raging at the time, so nobody really noticed this, and had chalked him up as missing, presumed dead.

Two days later, covered in soot, with a knot on his head the size of an eagle's egg, Blanchett had staggered into camp, clutching the teddy bear. It was ragged and moth-eaten and was missing an eye, which gave it a permanent squint. As teddy bears go, it would be difficult to find a more disreputable specimen. Nobody knew where he'd gotten it, and nobody was quite willing to ask.

The teddy bear, so far as Nessilka could tell, was now the brains of the pair. Blanchett refused to answer any query that was not directed at the bear, and only spoke when translating for the bear. In battle, the bear rode on top of his helmet.

It had been a long war. By that point, everybody had just figured it was easier to go along, particularly since Blanchett seemed rather more intelligent and helpful these days, under the bear's direction.

"He says okay," said Blanchett.

Nessilka nodded. Blanchett made the teddy bear salute and went off to get some sleep.

Weatherby stood up, tugging at his clothes, and said "Right, then! I'm—"

"Not tonight, Weatherby. There's a battle tomorrow."

Weatherby heaved a sigh. "Fine . . ."

"You can desert next week. That'll be fun, won't it?" *Gods*, thought Nessilka, listening to her own wheedling voice, *these troops don't need a sergeant, they need a babysitter.*

"Wanna desert *now* . . ." Weatherby muttered, slouching off to his tent. He kicked sullenly at a rock. Nessilka stared up at the sky and counted to ten.

She finally looked down, and then around the Nineteenth. Algol and Murray, her corporals. Thumper and Weatherby and the twins. Blanchett and his teddy bear. The half dozen others who didn't make trouble and just kept their heads down and tried to get through things. The great grim goblin gods only know who'd be alive after the battle tomorrow. All you could do was pray.

She wasn't very good at it—her prayers tended to sound like "You! Up there! Pay attention and heaven help you if you don't keep an eye on my boys!"—but as she had every night since becoming sergeant, Nessilka prayed.

The unicorn was gone, and the foal with her. Sings-to-Trees felt a moment of pure relief. The stall needed mucking out, but that was fine. He'd rather have mucked a dozen stalls than deal with a grumpy postpartum unicorn.

It was, all things considered, a glorious late spring morning. Birds sang in the trees, and the air was that tantalizing temperature that was just warm enough so it didn't feel like anything, until a delicious cool breeze would flicker across your skin. The leaves had come in brilliant, blinding green, and glittering like hot stained glass when the sun lanced through them.

Sings-to-Trees went around the side of the ramshackle barn, found his shovel, and went to work on the stall. It was hot work, lifting each shovelful into the wooden wheelbarrow, and he was sweating by the time he wheeled the first load up to the garden. Unicorn dung was pretty safe fertilizer. Sometimes the magical creatures had unusual things in their waste. He'd once nursed an injured peryton, a great gray stag with the wings of a heron and the carnivorous diet of a lion, for two weeks. He'd gone through a lot of chickens. Afterward, Sings put the dung on his tomato plants, and they'd grown six feet practically overnight. He could have handled *that*, but the fruit grew tiny green antlers. He could probably have handled *that*, too, even after they shed their velvet and got unsettlingly sharp, but he started finding the tomatoes gored and dripping seeds in the morning. Then the nearby zucchini began showing up with scarred rinds and suspicious gouges. Eventually he was down to one big eight-point tomato buck, a vicious vegetable he suspected was plotting to kill him. He'd put on his cockatrice-handling gloves and torn the whole patch out before things got out of hand.

He'd left that corner empty for a year, and then put in chard. Chard seemed pretty innocuous. Not a lot of mayhem available to chard. He didn't actually *like* chard, but there were plenty of animals that came through that would. So far it hadn't done anything suspicious. He shuddered to think what would have happened with potatoes.

The second wheelbarrow load came and went, and that was it. He sluiced the stones down with water and listened to it gurgle away, feeling the satisfaction of a dirty job done well.

A hoof stamped on the stones. He turned.

There was a dead deer looking at him.

He didn't yelp. On the scale of weird things that had come to him for help, this didn't even make the top ten. Still, he did inhale sharply, and he was glad the shovel was within easy reach.

It was a complete skeleton, fully articulated, standing framed in the square of light of the open barn door. Its filigreed shadow streamed away into the darkness of the barn and was lost.

He knew it was a deer because of the hooves and the skull and the build, but the delicacy of the thin bone legs was belied by the great rack of antlers on its head, a massive, labyrinthine rack, more than he'd known a deer could possibly fit onto its skull.

For one horrible moment, he wondered if thinking about the peryton had summoned its ghost—but no, there were no wings, and as far as he knew, the beast was still alive.

This creature was probably not alive. At least, not in the conventional sense.

It looked at him.

It didn't have eyes, and its empty eye sockets weren't full of eldritch fire, or even darkness. They were just eye sockets, full of ivory shadows and little more. Nevertheless, it looked at him.

"Can I help you?" he said.

It kept looking at him.

He spread his hands and took a cautious step forward, then another. It tilted its head, very slowly, and one hind hoof lifted a little, and scraped at the cobbles, the faintest sound, like a tree branch creaking in a soft breeze.

"Do you need help?" he tried again, and took another step.

It rattled at him. He froze.

The skeleton was articulated, so far as he could tell, by a kind of fine dark webbing at the joints. It looked almost like dried algae, brownish-black and forming organic loops and swirls over the balls of the joints. The deer had given a kind of rolling full-body shrug, down the length of its spine, and the clatter of vertebrae together had made the rattling noise he heard.

Sings lifted his hands, palms out. He didn't know what that was supposed to prove, if anything. No reason to think it would recognize any humanoid body language at all. It might understand him, or it might not—some of the odder creatures were able to understand human speech, and some were no different from regular beasts.

They stood there, for a few minutes, the man and the dead deer, and then it swung its head away, the long, smooth nasal bones pointing into the trees nearest the barn, and stamped its hoof again.

A skeletal doe melted out of the trees. She had an awkward, hopping gait, completely at odds with the ossuary grace of the buck. Sings could see immediately that her right front leg was broken. She held it hitched up in front of her, the naked hoof dangling awkwardly.

"Oh, you poor thing," he said and, quite forgetting the enormous buck standing there, started toward her.

A warning rattle stopped him. He turned and saw the buck eyeing him eyelessly, the head lowered just a little. He lifted his hands again.

"I'll do what I can," he told the bone stag. And then, hoping he wasn't about to be spread-eagled on that gigantic antlered mass, he bowed deeply to the stag.

And straightened.

And waited.

They stood there for a long moment. The leaves whispered in the trees, in a brief, cool breeze, that chilled the sweat on Sings-to-Trees's body.

The stag lifted its head.

Sings turned away. The skin between his shoulder blades crawled. He bowed to the doe, for good measure, and she gazed at him with empty eye sockets.

There was no flesh on her; there was nothing that could pull the face into any shape beyond the mute grin of a skull, but still, he thought he could see pain.

He knelt in front of her and very carefully took the injured leg in his hands.

He was shocked immediately by the warmth. This was no dead thing—this was *living* bone. The break was reasonably clean. He had wondered why, lacking muscle and skin to hold it in place, it hadn't just fallen off. Now he saw that the bones were threaded through and around with the black webbing, and a thick skein of it, through the hollow center, was still attached.

Hmm.

Had this been a real deer, he wouldn't have tried it. Such breaks were extremely difficult to fix—while setting the bone was straightforward enough, you had to keep them practically immobilized for weeks to keep them from breaking it again, and the captivity and stress killed them more surely than the break would. A wild deer could get by on three legs, and other than putting out food, there wasn't much you could do that wasn't worse than the injury. It was different with fawns. He could manage fawns, and although he couldn't return them to the wild, more than a few half-tame deer in parks in the elven city had started life on his farm.

This one, though . . . gods.

"I can splint it," he said to her, fairly sure she didn't understand him. "Splint it, and wrap it, and put some plaster on it. You'll have to stay off it if you can. You probably can't. Um." He was very aware of the stag's not-eyes boring into the back of his head.

"Let's start with that," he said, and got up. The stag rattled a little, then stopped, as if embarrassed. Walking backward, making "wait" gestures with both hands, he went inside the barn and began rummaging around for supplies with which to, once again, do the impossible.

War is just *not* efficient," said Murray.

This was such a typically Murray comment that Nessilka snorted with laughter, even under the circumstances.

They were standing in ranks on the top of the hill. Elves and humans stood in ranks at the bottom of the hill. In a few minutes, somebody was going to break and yell "Attack!" and the humans and elves would come up and the goblins would go down, and then it'd just be shouting and hitting and pointy things.

"Look at this," he continued. "They're going to charge up here, and we're going to beat them back, and at the end of the day, we'll probably still be up here, and they'll probably still be down there. We both know it. The battle isn't going to change anything, and it's all for control of this stupid hill, which neither of us would give a rat's hind end for if there wasn't a war."

"S'nice hill," rumbled Algol. "S'pretty, anyway." He had a wildflower tucked behind one ear.

"It's a trollslip," he said helpfully, when they all looked at him and his flower. "They grow on hillsides like this."

"It's very . . . um . . . pink," said Murray.

"My mom used to grow them back home."

There didn't seem to be anything more to say on that front. They all looked forward again.

He was right, so far as it went, but so was Murray. It was a hill, with big gray rocks scattered around the top, and little pink trollslips tumbling over them. Here and there, an oxeye daisy nodded in the sun. The hill had risen gently out of the woods below them, leaving the trees behind in favor of a band of heather, and the wildflowers. The other sides ranged between steepish (in front) and suicidal (to the sides.) It had a pleasant but not particularly dramatic view of the fields below.

A nice place for a picnic, maybe, but probably not a place you'd build a house.

Being the highest point for some miles, it was, however, the perfect place for a battle. Everybody wants the high ground, particularly if you're only four feet tall and need all the help you can get.

The elves down below looked like tall white foxes, all narrow pointy faces and broad pointy ears. Their pale silver hair floated around their heads like haloes. They stood in grim silent ranks and watched the goblins through narrowed eyes.

The humans below were a more varied lot and came in almost as many colors as goblins, from dark brown to pasty pink. No green, though. You couldn't trust a species that didn't come in green.

At least they fidgeted before the battle. Nessilka appreciated that. The elves stood like carved marble. The humans sweated and twitched and snickered and poked each other, very much like goblins.

"They say the waiting..."

"...is the worst part."

Mishkin and Mushkin had taken Algol's advice literally and were crowded up next to him like two ticks on a tomcat.

Algol considered this.

"Nah. The worst part is the bit where you hit the other guy and hope he doesn't hit you."

"Oh."

"And the bit where they hit you, that's the worst, too."

"...oh."

"And the bit where they've already hit you, and you're not sure if you're alive or not, that's definitely the wor—"

"Corporal!"

Algol blinked at Sergeant Nessilka. "Yes, Sarge?"

"It is possible to be *too* honest, Corporal."

"Yes, Sarge."

They all stood and fidgeted for a while.

"Do you think we could make tea?" asked Gladblack, who had a purple tint to his skin most of the time, but was now a kind of unhappy gray.

"No."

Weatherby was tugging at his clothes again. Behind Nessilka, Thumper was singing something tuneless under his breath. She caught something about "with a whack-whack here, and a whack-whack there..." and tuned him out.

"Do you think—" Murray began, and then there was no time for questions, because somebody had yelled "Charge!"

7

Nessilka had been in any number of battles, and she couldn't remember the first ten minutes of any of them.

She had a theory that if you could remember the first ten minutes, you'd never, ever charge at anybody again, so parts of your brain blotted them out.

The problem was that she couldn't imagine why her brain would want her to continue charging at people, and this then led her to the theory that parts of her brain worked for the Goblin High Command, which she didn't like at all.

Regardless, it was ten minutes into the battle, and she couldn't remember what had just happened. There'd been a lot of yelling. Everyone yelled. No matter what species you were, elf, human, goblin, orc, random bystander, you yelled. There had been a lot of hitting things. Her shield was bent in four or five places, and her arms ached dreadfully.

Algol went by at high speed, shield raised, with Mishkin and Mushkin practically stepping on his heels. Mishkin had gotten a sword from somewhere and was waving it dangerously close to Algol's kidneys.

She had no idea how the battle was going, but she didn't seem to be dead, so from her perspective, everything was really going rather well.

Unfortunately, Sergeant Nessilka had just seen a problem.

The problem stood on a little rise, just enough to lift him

out of the battle proper. He looked human, and he wasn't wearing armor or carrying any weapons.

He was doing something with his hands, and there was a blueness in the air around him—not really a blue light, per se, but the world around him was turning shades of blue, like something behind a pane of cobalt glass. That wasn't right. That was *magic*, that was.

A bolt of blueness streaked out from his open mouth and hit a knot of goblins, who fell down.

Aw, hell, Nessilka thought. *It's a wizard.*

ALL WIZARDS ARE crazy.

Not the quaint, colloquial "crazy" where you have an offbeat sense of humor and wear brightly colored socks, not mild eccentricity coupled with a general lack of fashion sense. Not "you don't have to be crazy to work here, but it helps." Wizards aren't weird. They are genuinely, legitimately, around the bend.

This is because magic is a form of psychosis.

Forget the bearded men wearing robes covered in stars trying to sell you bargain spellbooks. Nine times out of ten, it's a scam, and the tenth time, they really can do magic, but it's not something they can teach.

Various parties have done intensive studies of Arcane Manifestation Disorder, or AMD, and the results often make for interesting reading, but they still don't know what causes someone to have a sudden mental break and wake up able to throw fire from their fingertips. It just happens.

There are basically two kinds of sufferers of AMD—the high-functioning, and the rather less so. High-functioning wizards can live just fine on their own, and while they tend to be shy and awkward in social situations, and are easily startled, they're not any worse off than the rest of us.

The more unfortunate wizards generally require someone

to dress them and can't be allowed near any sharp objects.

By its very nature, magic is highly complex and highly individualized. It's hard to say what magic can and can't do, because it varies so wildly between wizards. Some of them are battle machines, some of them are good in the garden, some of them do weather. Some of them can, on a good day, turn mushrooms into hedgehogs, and some of them can shatter mountains. It's certainly not all *bad* things. A statue in Goblinhome commemorates Thurgle, who famously talked a nearby mountain out of erupting. There's a young woman in East Charring who doesn't talk, but can heal just about anything that ails you. You just don't know.

Because of this individuality, it's impossible to standardize magic. People have tried to set up wizarding schools, but rather than being charmingly quirky places with peculiar architecture, you just get a lot of very unhappy kids enduring puberty in an enclosed space, while wondering if their classmates are going to explode. While individuals with AMD often find work suited to their own particular talents, most governments find such unique skills—and people—hard to exploit, so the only large institutions with a policy of employing wizards en masse are various armies.

Sergeant Nessilka had been in the Goblin Army since she was old enough to lie about her age, and she had encountered a fair number of enemy wizards. There'd been the one who shot smothering clouds of butterflies out of his fingertips, and the one who made people's skeletons shuck off their bodies like someone taking off a heavy coat, and the really creepy one who'd just made people *go away*.

This guy shot blue out of his mouth. Nessilka had never seen anybody shoot blue from their mouths, but the goblins who'd been hit weren't getting up again, and that was more than enough for her.

"It's a wizard! Get the wizard!" somebody was yelling. "Follow me! Quick!" After a minute of this, Nessilka realized she was the one doing the yelling, and cursed her traitorous vocal cords. *Of all the body parts to suddenly discover patriotism...*

Then her feet appeared to discover it, as well, because she seemed to be charging at the wizard. *Why, feet? Why now? Why can't you be more like—oh, the spleen, say? The spleen never charges anybody!*

Her feet ignored her. Her vocal cords appeared to have gotten the hint, because she wasn't yelling any more, or perhaps her blood was just pounding in her ears too loudly to tell.

She wondered if anybody was actually following her.

Not daring to look behind her for fear of finding that she was making a suicide charge all on her own, she continued forward. The ground slipped and slid and squelched under her broad feet. At this stage of the fight, footing was often more dangerous than the other guys having swords—all those feet running and jumping and tearing over the hillside had churned it into dirt and mud and slippery bits. If you fell down, you slid, until you hit somebody else—a dead body if you were lucky, a live, angry body carrying a blunt instrument if you weren't.

Goblins actually have an advantage in this terrain since their feet are so huge, but there are limits. She tripped over something—*goodness, I hope that wasn't what it looked like*—and stumbled down the slope, not entirely in control of her own course.

An elf appeared in front of her. He had a sword. Unable to stop, and for lack of anything better to do, she ran directly into him, at full speed. He squawked and went down. So did she.

Overhead, another bolt of blue shot out and dropped a nearby goblin like a rock.

Sometimes whoever gets up first wins, and since Nessilka was sitting on the elf's legs, she had a tenuous advantage. The elf kicked and bucked under her. She slammed her club down on his knee, which put a stop to that, rolled to her feet, took aim, and stomped, hard.

Male elves are no different from any other humanoid species in some regards. He probably wouldn't die, but he'd certainly wish he had, and Nessilka didn't have time to stick around, with the wizard still spitting bolts of blue everywhere.

She slid and squelched forward. Then she got onto a patch that still had grass on it—*oh glory!*—and got traction and pounded forward.

She was twenty feet away, and it occurred to her that her entire plan was "hit wizard with club and hope for the best." This was not a bad plan, as such things go, but it did not seem to have a contingency for the wizard spitting blueness at her.

There were footsteps behind her. Somebody yelled.

The wizard looked up, and his eyes went wide.

Nessilka had to do it. She darted a glance behind her.

The entire Nineteenth Infantry, from Algol down to Blanchett's teddy bear, were right behind her.

Shock warred with gratitude warred with the horror that she was going to get them all killed. Nessilka left her emotions to sort the matter out on their own time, raised her club, and thundered up the last few feet to the wizard.

"Whooooohaaaaa!"

The wizard stopped shooting blue. His mouth opened again, but this time in what looked like a cry of terror, and he reached both hands to one side and grabbed at thin air.

Nessilka wondered briefly if he'd gone mad with terror or was trying to milk an invisible cow.

Then—and even for magic this was weird—he grabbed the air and *yanked*.

The air tore open—really tore, as if it were a big sheet of canvas with the world painted on it—and there was something on the other side. Darkness, shot with green, that *moved*.

Sergeant Nessilka did not know much about magic, but she was pretty sure that tearing holes in the air meant no good for anybody.

She tried to stop.

The Nineteenth Infantry, led by Algol, crashed into her back.

Her feet went out from under her, and she crashed into the wizard, who in turn crashed into the hole in the air.

The hole went "glorp!"

The wizard went "Arrrrgh!"

Nessilka went "Craaaap!"

Algol went "Sarge?"

The world went black.

Sings-to-Trees was tired, but he felt good. This was his normal state of being, so he didn't stop to notice it.

The bone doe, now with a splint and a tightly wrapped cast, had melted into the trees, followed by her brooding companion. The stag hadn't liked him messing around with the doe's leg and had rattled near-constantly, like a furious rattlesnake, until the doe had turned her head and snapped her exposed teeth in the stag's direction.

Sings-to-Trees gazed off in the middle distance with a vague, pleasant expression, the way that most people do when present at other people's minor domestic disputes, and after a moment, the stag had stopped rattling, and the doe had turned back and rested her chin trustingly on Sings-to-Trees's shoulder.

This would have been a touching gesture, if her chin hadn't been made of painfully pointy blades of bone. It was like being snuggled by an affectionate plow.

But the leg had gotten splinted and wrapped, and the doe was walking more easily on it already, and beyond that, it was in the hands of whatever gods looked after the articulated skeletons of deer.

He pulled on the rusted handle of the pump until water gushed out. He washed his hands, then plunged his whole head briefly under it. Refreshed and spluttering, he headed back up to the farmhouse to look something up.

Sings-to-Trees, while not having many fragile things, did own a small library which he kept locked in a cedar chest for safekeeping. One look at the outside of the chest—it was scorched by fire, scored by claws, chewed by teeth, and some kind of acid had etched a random design in the lid—made it obvious why something as fragile as paper was on the inside.

He had several herbals, full of small, neat drawings of plants and careful notes (some of which he'd written himself). He had *Sleestak's Guide to Common Farmyard Maladies*, and *Diseases of the Goat*, (it was amazing how many of those showed up in trolls) and *Thee Goode Elf's Alamanack* (which contained many, many 'E's, and not much useful information), and the exhaustive *Herbal Remedies*, which was six inches thick and full of bookmarks. He even had a dog-eared copy of *Medica Magica*, which was full of outright lies and falsehoods, but every now and then had something worth paying attention to.

The book he really wanted was near the bottom. Sings-to-Trees dug down, building up precarious stacks of leather bindings on either side of the trunk, until he found the volume and lifted it into the light.

The silver leaf had long since flaked off the cover, and the letters had become a series of flat spaces in a sea of tooled leather, read as much with the hand as the eye. In the language of humans, it read *Bestiary*.

The elf sat down and began turning pages carefully.

There was no index. The author had been a wizard who had clearly seen some terrible things, and had been doing well to hold it together long enough to write the descriptions, which were rambling in places and painfully abrupt in others, when they weren't downright illegible. There were no chapters, and nothing resembling alphabetical order. The entries showed up where they showed up, and given the nature of some of the comments interspersing the text, the reader was generally grateful to get that much.

The pictures, though . . . the pictures practically moved on the page. Even in scratchy black and white, they shone like little gems. The elegant neck of the unicorn flexed, the serpentine mane of the catoblepas writhed, muscles pulsed in the shoulders of the great boar.

Magic may have been involved. Sings-to-Trees rather thought that the author's gift had been visions, because the creatures gave every evidence of being drawn from life, and in some cases, like the kraken or the ice-moles, that would have been quite a feat.

He was two-thirds of the way through the book, scrutinizing each illustration carefully, before he saw it.

The carefully articulated skeleton of a stag gazed back at him from the page.

". . . thee cervidine or cervidian does range widely through the wold, being in all ways like unto a true deer, saving that it be made of Bones and not of Flesh. (Whyfor are you poking at me? Stop! Stop, I implore you!) The cervidian reproduces by manner unknown, though it is said that they may build a fawn of bones, and so imbue it with essential life (the poking to cease! To cease!), but I have not been witness to this and consider it may be folly. It is known the cervidian is much fond of magic and very curious, like unto a magpie, and will oft be found in areas of great mystical disturbance, which perhaps it may eat, for it takes no sustenance of grass (I will become angry if there is more poking!) and only damps its bones in water and dew. (Why do you not stop . . . ?!)"

It went on in that vein for quite a while, and by the time the author had gotten control of himself again, he was talking about the limerick contests held by manticores.

Sings-to-Trees closed the book thoughtfully. Of course, just because the cervidian was attracted by magical disturbance, it didn't follow that there was one happening nearby, but it was still . . . interesting. He hadn't seen such a creature in all the years he'd been out here.

He should probably send a pigeon to the rangers and ask them if anything weird was happening.

There was an almighty crash from the hearth. Sings-to-Trees bolted to his feet.

The raccoon had learned how to open the hutch and had celebrated its newfound freedom by knocking the hutch over, along with the iron fire grate and the tea kettle that had been warming there. It sat in the midst of the wreckage, paws clasped in glee, and greeted Sings-to-Trees with a happy "Clur-r-r-r-p."

The elf sighed. He had enough trouble without borrowing more. He scooped up the raccoon cub, rescued the kettle, and began putting books away before his patient got any more bright ideas.

THE SERGEANT'S HEAD hurt.

Somebody was singing under their breath. Thumper again, probably. "With a whack-whack here . . ." Gods, her head hurt. She wanted to go back to sleep. Sleep was good.

"Sarge?"

Oh, lord. They wanted her to wake up.

"Sarge, we have a problem."

Worse and worse. They wanted her to wake up and be the sergeant.

She didn't *want* to wake up and be the sergeant. Being the sergeant was thankless, and they didn't pay you very much more, and when something went wrong, you were the one that had to fix things. Responsibility was lousy.

"Sarge . . ."

On the other hand, if you didn't see things were done right, it'd get done badly, and watching the resulting inefficiency was like being poked repeatedly in a sore tooth. It galled at her.

Besides, if she didn't get up, Murray would be in charge, and he hadn't done anything bad enough to deserve that.

She opened one eye. Algol was shaking her shoulder.

"Ungghffff . . ."

That didn't sound right. She paused, licked her lips, tried again. Her mouth was dry. "Yes, Corporal?"

"Um, we have a problem, Sarge."

Of course they had a problem. Everybody always had a problem. There was a war on, after all.

She sat up.

"Where's the battle?"

"We don't seem to be there any more, Sarge."

"Don't seem to . . ." Nessilka looked around.

Most of the Nineteenth Infantry was sprawled on the ground. Murray was on the other side of what looked like a small clearing in the woods, except they'd been on a hillside, not in the woods. Where had the woods come from?

"Did these trees grow while I was asleep?"

Algol considered this dutifully. "I think they take longer than that, Sarge."

"Is the battle over? Did you carry me back the way we came?"

Algol shook his head. "I just woke up, Sarge."

Murray came over, folding up a little glass and brass contraption in his hands. "We're not at the battlefield."

"Thank you, Corporal Obvious," said Nessilka, ignoring that she had said something similar about half a minute before.

"No, Sarge, you don't understand. We're not anywhere near the battlefield. We're miles off. There's a break in the trees over there, and I got a sighting on a mountain. I think it's Goblinhome."

"Well, that's fine, then," said Nessilka. "I mean, Goblinhome—"

"Sarge, it's at least fifty miles away. We're on the wrong side of it."

She considered this.

"The sea side?"

"The *human* side, Sarge."

Sergeants don't scream. They shout at people quite a lot, but they do not scream. Nessilka took a deep breath, and let it out cautiously. She didn't scream. Okay. That was fine, then.

"So what you're saying is . . . we're behind enemy lines."

Murray laughed. There was a slightly hysterical edge to it. "Sarge, we'd have to move about forty miles up to just be behind enemy lines. We're practically behind the enemy *nation.*"

"Ah."

There was a long moment, while Murray fiddled with his glass and brass thing, and Algol stared up into the trees, and Nessilka's mind was an absolute blank. She was a sergeant by virtue of always being the responsible one. She'd had the same two weeks of boot camp as everybody else. At no point had they covered what to do when you are accidentally whisked into the heart of enemy territory.

Still, you had to do something.

"All right," she said finally. "Murray, Algol, get everybody awake and on their feet. Check for wounded. See who came with us."

They saluted and peeled off. Nessilka got to her feet and looked around.

It wasn't a bad forest. Other than the fact that they absolutely weren't supposed to be there, it was a perfectly nice forest. It was deep and green, and the ground was covered in a soft mat of some little plant or other. The spots under the trees were deep with pine needles and leaf litter. Birds were calling from the canopy. The branches whispered and shifted gently in the wind.

It was a nice forest. It had probably belonged to goblins once. It was a shame they couldn't stay here for a bit. She sighed. Up in the trees, a crow went "ark!" and the call seemed to hang in the air for a long time.

"Everybody's up, Sarge," said Murray. "Nobody's bad hurt, but Blanchett's got a twisted ankle."

"He says I can walk on it," said Blanchett, nodding to the teddy bear. "Probably not a full march, though."

"Tell him thank you," said Nessilka absently.

About two-thirds of the Whinin' Niners had come through the hole in the air with her. Algol, Murray, Blanchett, Thumper, the recruits—gods, the recruits—plus Gloober, who always had a finger in some orifice or other, and Weasel, who was tiny and slender and who stuttered when you tried to talk to her. Everybody else was back at the battlefield.

"And we found the wizard, too," said Algol.

"Oh, dear."

The wizard was in a lot worse shape than any of them. He was still unconscious, his breathing was shallow, and his skin was gray. This would have been normal in a goblin, but he was one of the pinkish humans, so it probably wasn't a good sign. He had a thin, worried face and badly bitten fingernails. He didn't look like an unstoppable killing machine, but then, who did?

There didn't seem to be any marks on him, and Nessilka was pretty sure she hadn't run into him that hard.

"It's probably the magic," said Murray. "I bet he was trying to cut and run—that thing in the air was an escape route. Maybe it takes energy to go through it, and when we all fell through it, it knocked him out."

"What do we do . . ."

". . . with him now?" asked the recruits meekly.

The Nineteenth all looked at each other, while carefully not meeting each other's eyes, which was a pretty neat trick.

Nessilka sighed.

They ought to kill him. They all *knew* they ought to kill him. He was the Enemy, and he was a wizard, and he'd probably killed a lot of goblins shooting that blue stuff out of his mouth. He'd probably kill them all if he had a chance.

The problem was that it's one thing to kill somebody when they're charging at you with a sword, or shooting blue things, but it's an entirely different thing to kill somebody who's lying unconscious on the ground. The one is just war. Wars are like that.

This, though . . . this felt like murder.

Goblins are nasty and smelly and grumpy and have bad attitudes, but they're not inherently *bad*. They're pretty much like anybody else. They don't kill people for fun, regardless of what the propaganda posters say. And this guy was a wizard, and wizards were scary, but you had to feel a little sorry for them, too. They probably hadn't wanted to wake up one day with the power to unmake the world.

Nessilka shook her head. "We're not going to kill him."

Everybody relaxed imperceptibly.

"We can't tie him up, though," Murray pointed out. "When he wakes up, if he gets his hands or his mouth free, he could magic us."

"So we'd better be a long way off when he wakes up," said Nessilka. "Everybody, get ready to move out. Thumper, cut a crutch for Blanchett. Gloober, get your finger out of there. Algol, do we have any blankets?"

"No, Sarge. We don't have much. Nobody took their full kit into the battle. Murray's got some mechanical stuff in his pack, and I've got a rope, but beyond that, it's basically whatever we've got on our backs, and our field kits."

The standard issue goblin field kit is a pocket knife, two bandages of dubious cleanliness, a rubber band, a stump of candle, some dried fruit, and a book of matches. It fits into the standard issue tin cup, which then fits into a small pouch. It was better than nothing, but not by much.

"If I cannibalize a coupla things"—Murray patted his pack, which caused everyone to brace briefly for an explosion— "I can probably rig another travel stove. We'll be able to cook, anyway."

"Does anybody have a bow and arrow?"

Nobody did. Archers were another unit entirely. The Nineteenth was strictly hand-to-hand.

Weasel put up a hand shyly.

"Yes, Private?"

"I c-c-c . . ." Weasel turned bright red.

Nessilka put an arm around the small goblin's shoulders and turned her around so that the eyes of the troop weren't on her. "In your own time, Private."

"I c-can use a s-s-sling, S-s-sarge."

"Good. We might actually eat after all."

"We're almost ready, Sarge," said Algol. Blanchett was experimenting with his crutch, under the watchful eye of the teddy bear.

Nessilka looked down at the wizard. No blankets. She sighed.

She was going to miss it tonight, but she pulled her cloak off and laid it over the wizard. Poor sod was probably in shock, and if he didn't stay warm, it was as good as having killed him. Besides, he was a war-wizard, and whatever the army did to them, it sure didn't make them any happier or better at fending for themselves. "Algol, see if you can get a little water into him before we go. I'd rather not leave a trail of dead bodies behind us."

Algol nodded.

"Everybody else—I want to get at least five miles away from here, and then we're looking for a place to hole up for a bit that's hidden and defensible. Let's try not to leave a trail like a wounded moose, okay?"

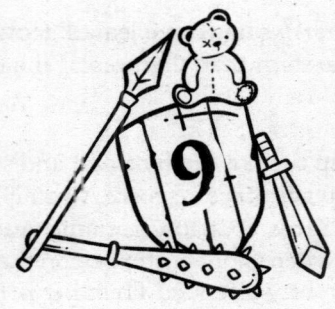

It was a beautiful day in the forest. The birds were calling. The birds were calling a lot.

Nessilka was getting a feeling that whatever they were calling was probably the ornithological equivalent of "Come get a load of *this*!"

Traveling through thick woods with a troop of goblins is not unlike a nature hike with a group of grumpy toddlers with weapons.

They fell into things. They fell out of things. They attacked bushes. The bushes frequently attacked back. They startled small animals, who startled them badly in return, causing them to fall over into more bushes. They stepped on things that were not good to step on, and stepped in things that squelched, or stank, or exploded with spores.

Sergeant Nessilka watched as her troop discovered a patch of poison oak, and had to look away.

Blanchett stumped up beside her, leaned on his crutch, and eyed the rest of the troop.

"He says that's poison oak they're rolling in," he informed her, pointing to the teddy bear.

"I think he's right."

Murray emerged from the thicket, holding a sprig of leaves at arm's length.

"Leaves of three . . ." Murray was muttering. "Leaves of

three . . . gods! *Everything* has three leaves! How do you *tell*?"

"If you touch me with that, Corporal, I'll have you court-martialed."

"Yes, Sarge."

They rounded up the now-itchy troop and staggered on.

"How far do you think we've come, Murray?"

"Maybe a mile, Sarge. Probably not much more than that. We lost some time when Gloober stepped on the wasp's nest."

A tree had apparently offended Thumper in some fashion. He attacked it with his maces, and then with his teeth.

"Algol, go rescue that tree. Gloober, if you've got poison ivy on that finger, you're going to regret sticking it in there. Weasel—whoa!"

Weasel turned scarlet and mumbled something.

"Is that a *pheasant*?"

"I m-made a s-s-sling, S-sarge." She held out a strip that, in a former life, had been a section of rancid goat-hide loincloth. Slung over her shoulder was a very large, very dead bird, nearly as big as the little goblin's torso and sporting a gorgeous rainbow of feathers. "I th-thought—"

"Weasel, remind me to put in for a medal for you when we get home. Bird tonight! Can you catch another one?"

The little goblin mumbled and shrugged and stared at her toes.

"Do your best. Make someone else carry the bird."

"Sarge, there's a break in the trees up ahead." Murray was already digging in his backpack. "Permission to go scout the land."

"Permission granted. What do you call that contraption, anyway?"

"What, the looky-tube-thing?"

"Yeah."

"The looky-tube-thing."

"Ask a stupid question . . . Yeah, go get the lay of the land. Everybody, take five. Gloober, I warned you about that finger!"

MURRAY RETURNED IN about ten minutes, frowning. Algol supervised the application of mud to scrapes, stings, and welts. Nessilka was mentally composing a report to the Goblin High Command detailing the need for wilderness survival training for the troops.

Heading One—Poison Oak, identification of . . .

"What's the good word, Murray?"

Murray chewed on his lower lip. "Not much of a good word. We're on the west edge of a pretty substantial forest. It runs a fair way, and it curves around to the north, so if we follow the edge, we'll get closer to Goblinhome, but not very fast."

"What about striking out from the forest?"

"Don't recommend it, Sarge. It's all farmland out there between us and home—absolutely flat for a long way, practically right up to the foothills. At least thirty miles of farm, twenty more of hills. You or I could make it in a coupla days, but with this crew—" He spread his hands in an eloquent gesture that expressed, rather better than words, the general competence of the Whinin' Niners at anything resembling stealth. "Better part of a week, in the open, with cornfields and hedgerows for cover. You know I'll follow you anywhere, Sarge, but I think it's suicide."

Heading Two—Moving stealthily, practice thereof . . .

"And if we follow the forest?"

"Probably closer to fifty or sixty miles, although it's hard to tell. Could be more. We'll still have an open bit at the end—can't tell if the woods go up to the foothills, but I don't think they do—but we'd be under cover most of the way."

Nessilka nodded. She had a brief vision of herding the Nineteenth across open fields by night, hiding in drainage ditches during the day, barking dogs, men with crossbows, and shuddered. "I'm thinking we'll go with your plan."

"One more thing. There's a town—probably ten miles

north, real close to the woods. We can probably go deeper in and go around it, and risk getting lost, but we might want to try raiding it."

"Raiding? Corporal, there are *nine* of us." Nine goblins could, on a good day, probably disrupt a child's tea party or decimate a chicken coop, but Nessilka wouldn't have put them against anything bigger.

"I'm not suggesting we try to pillage the town, Sarge. I had more in mind hitting a henhouse, and maybe somebody's laundry. Have you seen Thumper's loincloth?"

"Thank you, I've been trying not to look."

"There's a coupla isolated farmhouses on the outskirts. I think a small group could raid one."

"I've got no stomach for killing farmers, Murray, and if we do, we're going to have hunters after us before you can say "glarguk.""

"Great gods, no, Sarge, I'm hoping they won't even see us."

She relented. "Okay, talk to me again when we've found a place to hole up for a bit. I'm still hoping to put miles between us and that wizard."

IN THE END, they found a kind of dirt cave in a mostly dried-out riverbed. If it rained, they might flood out, but the promise of even a muddy pool of water nearby was more than enough to recommend the campsite. They had made at least three miles, which wasn't as much as Nessilka liked, but it was better than nothing.

Weasel had managed to bring down a rabbit. A rabbit and a bird weren't much between nine people, but along with the dried field rations, it wasn't bad, and everybody knew it could have been a lot worse. Both rabbit and pheasant were cooked on a spit and were greeted with so many appreciative complaints—"Gah! Tough as an old shoe!" "You call this rabbit? Looks like a long-eared ferret. Tastes like one, too!" "What was this bird eating, stinkbugs?"—that the little goblin was completely tongue-tied.

"Okay, guys, tomorrow we're doing a full day's march," said Nessilka once the last bones had been gnawed. Groans greeted this. She waved them off. "We've got a route back to Goblinhome, but we're sticking to the woods for now."

"How far are we . . ."

". . . from Goblinhome, Sarge?"

"'Bout fifty miles as the crow flies. We're not crows, though, so we're looking at seventy or eighty."

More groans. "Why can't we take the short way?"

"'Cause it's through human farmland, and I don't think they'll be real happy to see us."

"Perhaps we could go in disguise?" asked Gloober hopefully.

"We're four feet tall and *green*. I think they're going to notice."

Blanchett consulted with his teddy bear for a few minutes, and then said, "He says it's a good plan, Sarge." The teddy bear had one of the pheasant tail feathers stuck behind one ear, giving it a jaunty look.

"Err . . . thank him for me." Nessilka wondered briefly what she'd have done if the teddy bear hadn't approved, had a brief vision of a mutiny led by a one-eyed stuffed animal, and squelched it. It had been a long enough day already.

It was a long night, too.

Goblins are good at sleeping on the ground. They had all been doing it for so long that they hardly cared any more—pack for a pillow, cloak if they had one. And tonight they had the luxury of cut pine boughs for a mattress, which was significantly better than camping on the hillside. No one was complaining there.

No, the problem was the noises.

Generally the noises of goblin digestion, snoring, and other indelicate processes were enough to drown out anything outside. This time, however, the gurgle of nine stomachs had nothing on the woods.

"Those aren't normal," said Thumper, the fourth or fifth time something went by with a *swoosh* outside, as if on enormous wings.

"It's owls," said Murray.

"It's not owls," said Thumper. "I'm a forest goblin, 'kay? Those aren't owls."

"You can't have been in the forest since you were little," said Murray.

"They haven't changed owls since I was a kid. Owls are silent, like. They sneak up on stuff. That's *not* an owl."

As if exhausted by speaking this many words all at once, he fell silent. Everybody listened.

Something that probably wasn't an owl whooshed by again.

"We don't like this, Sarge," said Mishkin and Mushkin.

"Sarge doesn't like it either," said Nessilka, "but it's out there and we're in here, and it'll have to come through me to get to you, so go to sleep."

She was closest to the entrance of the cave, and she'd always had pretty good hearing. She was probably the only one who could hear the other noise—the soft, sucking sound of footsteps in mud, as something walked quietly up the riverbed, fifteen or twenty feet away.

Thhhhwuck. Thhhhwuck.

Swoosh.

She glanced behind her. Murray was the next closest, but he was half-deaf from his time in the Mechanics Corps and the daily explosions. She didn't say anything.

Her hand tight on the handle of the club, Sergeant Nessilka stared wide-eyed into the dark.

SINGS-TO-TREES STOOD ON his porch, a cup of tea in one hand, and frowned into the darkness.

He wasn't particularly scared of the dark. He knew most

of what lurked in it and had occasionally removed thorns from their paws. And although he was careful never to rely on it, he was fairly certain that there was an understanding among the smarter denizens of the forest that he and his farm were off-limits. He suspected he'd been lumped in with the little birds that pick the teeth of crocodiles, something too useful to waste on a whim.

For the predators that went on two legs, there were always the trolls. A desperate man had come to the farm once, and he'd been much more desperate after the trolls got him cornered on the roof and the gargoyle sat on his head. He'd been positively grateful to see the rangers when they came to take him away.

Sings-to-Trees had lived out here for years, more or less by himself, and never had any particular cause to fear the dark.

Still . . .

There was something odd about the dark tonight.

The elf wrapped his fingers in Fleabane's ruff. The coyote whined briefly.

He must feel it too.

Sings-to-Trees wished he could put his finger on it. The crickets all sang the usual songs, and the fireflies had been out in force through the evening. The spring peepers had mostly stopped peeping, but that was nothing more sinister than the season passing. Early cicadas had begun to take their place.

It wasn't too quiet. It was a healthy forest at night, so it was downright noisy. The stars were in the usual positions, and the leaves were hissing the way that leaves always hiss in the wind.

Still, something was making him uneasy.

Fleabane sighed and flopped against his shins. The coyote's hackles kept coming up, then easing back down. Sings-to-Trees knew exactly how he felt.

The leaves sighed. The crickets chirped. A lone firefly, still lovelorn, flashed its message to any other fireflies that might be looking for a good time.

The bone deer picked their way across his memory. *Attracted to mystical disturbance.* Hmmm.

He wondered what a mystical disturbance looked like. He hoped it didn't feel like this.

On the roof, the gargoyle mumbled something deep in its chest, a gravelly sound of unease. Fleabane whined again.

A leaf insect made its way slowly across one of the porch pillars, its body shadowy green in the light from the doorway. Sings-to-Trees watched it pick its way along, one spindly leg at a time, until it was out of sight.

Still nothing had happened. Still the crickets sang.

The gargoyle's footsteps paced back and forth across the roof.

Eventually, for lack of anything better to do, Sings-to-Trees went inside and barred his door against the dark.

The next day was easier. The Whinin' Niners had finally gotten their heads around the fact that they were here, in the woods, and not on the battlefield. Goblins are nothing if not adaptable. Fewer bushes were engaged in combat. Everyone had learned to recognize poison oak, and Thumper had remembered how to spot a few kinds of edible berry. Most of them weren't ripe yet, so breakfast was a painfully sour affair, but it beat starvation.

They walked. They stopped occasionally to drink at streams and soak their hot, sore feet, but never for very long.

Nessilka kept a grueling pace to start. It wasn't just a desire to keep the wizard behind her, although that was part of it. Mostly, it was the tracks that she'd found in the mud this morning.

They'd looked a bit like hoof prints. Actually, they'd looked a lot like hoof prints, except that most hooved animals did not have claws. She'd always thought the two were mutually exclusive, in fact, but unless they'd been stalked by a deer wearing fighting spurs, she didn't have a better explanation.

She'd stamped them out—no sense causing a panic—but she didn't want to be anywhere near the owner of the tracks when they stopped tonight.

Murray seemed pensive. He kept turning his head

and staring into the woods, a line forming between his eyebrows, and muttering something to himself. Nessilka watched him do this for the better part of an hour until the quiet muttering started to get on her nerves.

"Okay, Murray, you're a genius. What do you think?"

Murray grimaced. "Sorry, Sarge."

"Didn't ask you to be sorry. I want to know what you think."

"I don't like it, Sarge." He made a grasping gesture with one hand, as if trying to pluck an answer out of the air. "There's *something* about these woods. I can't quite place it. I'm not seeing the right thing. I'm a marsh goblin. I don't know quite what I'm looking for. But there's something that's . . . off."

"Thumper's a forest goblin. Ask him."

Murray started to shrug dismissively, and then stopped. "Maybe you're right. Hey, Thumper!"

Thumper dropped back to walk next to them. "Mm?"

"Tell me what's wrong with these woods."

Thumper's brow furrowed deep enough to plant corn. "Wrong? There's nothin' wrong with it. S'perfectly good woods." He reached out and patted the bark of a passing tree. "Lookit the size of this fellow! Probably half-rotted out. Ant nests. Wasps, too, I bet. Come down in the next big storm and kill us all. Wonderful old tree."

Murray shook his head, making the grasping gesture again. "No—no—*almost*—crud! Thumper, what kinds of trees are these?"

"Looks like oak mostly. Good oaks, not those wretched little pin oaks. Some big pines, but not many. Saw some cedar a while back."

"Wrong question, wrong question . . ." muttered Murray, plucking at the air again.

"What's the right question?" asked Nessilka.

Murray made a quick silencing motion that was a little rude to use on a superior officer, but Nessilka wasn't going to interfere with genius at work.

"I'm not seeing something. I'm not seeing something because it isn't there . . . Thumper, how old is that tree?"

Thumper shrugged. "Coupla hundred years. I'd have to cut it down and count rings to say for—"

Murray's hand shot out and grabbed the air as if he'd caught a rope. "Cut it down! That's it! They aren't cutting it down! Thumper, how long since this area was logged?"

"Logged?" Thumper shook his head. "This is, y'know, peak forest, the old stuff. It hasn't been logged in the last thousand years."

"Yes! That's it! That's what's wrong!"

"You'd rather somebody cut it all down?" asked Thumper stiffly. "Fine. What I'd expect out of a marsh goblin . . ."

"No, no, no! That's just it!" Murray was practically dancing. "Sarge, they haven't cut any trees! There's a human town right over there, practically, *and they haven't cut any trees!*"

"That's a little weird," admitted Nessilka. "Even we cut trees."

"Exactly! They need wood for houses and fences and wagons and firewood and all kinds of stuff! But, Sarge, they haven't touched this forest at all! Why not?"

"Maybe they think it's haunted?" asked Nessilka, thinking of the clawed hoofprints and the whooshers.

Murray shook his head. "I doubt it. Not when it's the only source of wood for miles. No. There's only one reason people don't cut down a forest. Somebody already owns it. And who lives in forests?"

Nessilka felt a cold prickling crawl down her spine. "You mean—"

Murray nodded. "*Elves . . .*"

THEY KEPT WALKING.

There is only so long that you can clutch your weapons and wait for white-faced figures to leap from behind the trees. For the Whinin' Niners, this was about forty-five minutes. Maybe there were elves. If there were, they'd probably find out soon enough. In the meantime, poison oak was a more immediate concern, and harder to spot.

Nessilka called a halt in the late afternoon. "Okay, everybody take five." She looked around the Whinin' Niners and sighed.

Most of them were doing okay, but the two recruits and Blanchett were about done in. The recruits were just not used to sustained marching, but poor Blanchett was gray-faced and sweating from having to cover the irregular terrain on his crutch.

"Blanchett, sit down before you fall down. Yes, that goes for the bear, too. Mishkin, Mushkin, sit. Murray, you still want to try raiding a farmhouse?"

Murray nodded.

"Okay. Murray, you're in charge. Algol, Gloober, go with Murray. Don't take any unnecessary risks. I'd rather nobody saw you at all. Stealth is more important than clean clothes."

She wracked her brain for anything else useful to say.

"Gloober, get your finger out of there."

They waited.

"And good luck."

The three saluted and moved off toward the fields.

"Weasel, you and Thumper go see if you can't find something to eat, and keep your eyes peeled for anything that might make a good campsite. The rest of us will wait here."

The pair saluted. Nessilka watched them go, the tiny little Weasel and the slab of muscle that was Thumper.

"Okay, troops," she said, turning back to Blanchett and the twins. "You three rest up. That's an order. Blanchett, will the bear mind if I borrow your helmet?"

There was a brief consultation. "He says it's okay, Sarge."

"Good. I could really use some tea."

MAKING TEA IN a used orc helmet recently converted to teddy bear sedan chair was an experience, but good sergeants learn to improvise. The hard part was getting the helmet clean. Who knew that Blanchett was using so much hair gel under that thing?

She had just gotten the water boiling when she heard a rustling in the bushes.

It was Murray. He and Algol and Gloober emerged from the woods, looking thoughtful. (Well, Murray and Algol looked thoughtful. Gloober had his finger up his nose again.)

"That was quick," she said.

Murray tugged at his ponytail. "Sarge . . . I think you better come look at this."

"What is it?"

"There's nobody there."

She raised her eyebrows. "That's good, right? They stepped out. We can grab the laundry and nobody'll be the wiser."

"No, Sarge, I don't think they stepped out. I think . . ."

He fell silent.

Algol put a hand on her arm. "Sarge," he rumbled, "you *really* better come look at this."

"Okay. Gloober, stay here. Everybody, lay low, keep quiet, don't start any large fires." She cast around for the next most responsible person on the chain of command and sighed. Oh well, no help for it. "Blanchett, the bear's in charge."

He made the bear salute. "He says he's honored by your trust, Sarge!"

Nessilka nodded. *He can't be any worse than some of the generals . . .*

"Let's go."

Sings-to-Trees had finally finished every small chore to be done around the farm, and by mid-afternoon, too.

This was so unusual that he sank down into the rocking chair on the porch with his eyes closed, because he was fairly sure that the moment he opened them, he would see something he'd forgotten, and then he'd have to get up again.

Fleabane ambled over and flopped down at his feet. Sings-to-Trees dangled a hand over the arm of the chair, and the coyote dragged a long tongue over his fingers.

The elf was content to slouch in the chair for a few minutes, feeling the afternoon sun baking his face and forearms.

Sometimes, even though he was fairly young as elves go, the whole thing got away from him. Too many animals, too many injuries, too many things that needed to get done right this minute. He occasionally wished for an assistant. Unfortunately, humans weren't all that interested in sending their young to live with an elf, and the other elves... he knew well enough what they thought. He was like some kind of martyr, as far as they were concerned. They were glad he existed, but nobody wanted to get too close, for fear of getting unicorn crap or something worse on them.

Sometimes he thought about giving it all up, moving into the glade and taking up something respectable, like glass-whispering.

In a few hundred years, when he was ancient and his knees creaked like old floorboards, did he really want to be tottering around the farm, midwifing unicorns and bandaging trolls?

He opened his eyes with a sigh, and a troll was looking at him.

Sings-to-Trees didn't quite yelp, but he made a choked noise. Fleabane's tail thumped companionably on the boards. The coyote liked trolls. They brought goat meat, and Fleabane was desperately fond of goat.

The troll was sitting on the path, and spilling over on the sides. He recognized it as Frogsnoggler—that wasn't the troll's real name, but it was the closest phonetic equivalent to the complicated set of sounds that it used to describe itself.

At least, he thought it was describing itself. He had never been able to learn their language. Fortunately, they understood his perfectly well.

"You gave me quite a start," the elf said, getting up. The troll's silent approach didn't surprise him—trolls moved with eerie silence for their size—but seeing one out and about before sunset was unusual.

"Grah!" said the troll, and smiled. Trolls were always smiling. Their mouths were wide and froglike and naturally suited to it. With its eyes squeezed tight against the sunlight, Frogsnoggler looked comically pleased.

"What are you doing up at this hour, anyway?" Sings-to-Trees asked, coming down from the porch.

The troll's face fell. "Grah..." it said humbly, and held out its arms.

"Oh, *no*..."

Cradled against its chest, almost lost against the clay-colored bulk, lay a battered gray fox. An ugly leg trap, all steel fangs and metal, hung grotesquely from one small back leg.

"Grah?" asked the troll anxiously, holding out the injured fox. "Grah?"

Sings-to-Trees got his arms under the fox, who snapped

weakly at him. The trap hit his chest with a metallic clunk. Outrage choked him. "Bloody poachers!" he growled, shifting his grip on the fox. The trap chattered again.

"Grah!" agreed the troll. Its low forehead wrinkled in a frown. Immense tusks glittered briefly at the edges of its mouth.

Sings-to-Trees took a deep breath and let the anger go. There were more important matters at hand. The fox was a skinny little thing, panting in pain and probably dehydration as well, and standing around with his teeth gritted didn't do the poor creature any good.

First things first . . .

He wasn't strong enough to get the leg trap off himself, but fortunately, brute strength was squatting at arm's-length. "Okay, Frogsnoggler, I'm going to need your help."

"Grug!" It nodded vigorously.

"I'll hold him. I want you to pull the trap open—slowly!—and I'll see if we can get the leg out without something worse happening."

The fox's leg was badly cut but not crushed. The little animal had been lucky. Sings-to-Trees tossed a towel over its head to keep it from ripping his arm open, held the fox's torso firmly under his elbow, and nodded to the troll. "Carefully, now . . ."

Frogsnoggler reached down and opened the steel trap as casually as Sings-to-Trees might open a book. The elf pulled the fox's foot free, working as delicately as he could to keep the wound from being torn even wider by the cruel metal teeth. The fox panted in pain.

It took less than a minute, but several subjective eternities passed for Sings-to-Trees.

"Got it . . . got it . . . There!" He reached out and patted Frogsnoggler's flank with his free hand. "Well done!"

The troll beamed at him. "Grah! Grah-grah-hrragggh?"

Sings-to-Trees had no idea what the troll had said, but he could venture a guess. "I think he'll probably be fine, but I need to treat this. Can you help me a little more? If the daylight's not bothering you too much?"

"Grah, grah." The troll waved a hooflike hand dismissively.

"Then if you could take him..." Sings-to-Trees placed the fox back into the troll's arms and went to get catgut and a needle.

Cleaning the wound and sewing the fox's leg up was a tedious process for Sings-to-Trees, and an undoubtedly painful one for the fox, despite the sedative the elf poured down its throat. He was rather glad the troll was holding the animal. The fox kept snapping and trying to thrash, but it might as well have been held down by a mountain.

"One more ... and ... there we go." He tied off the thread. "Okay. I'll keep him for a few days and make sure it heals up clean, and he gets a couple of square meals." He accepted the fox again. "Thank you and—oh, no!"

"Grah?"

Sings-to-Trees leveled an accusing finger at Frogsnoggler. "Why didn't you tell me he was biting you?"

"Grah..." The troll shrugged and scuffed the dirt with one hoof, like a small child caught at mischief. Its left arm was full of tooth marks, most of which had skidded off the thick hide, but a few were filling up with blood.

"Stay right there. I'm cleaning those."

"Graww..."

The fox went into an empty hutch, most recently home to an infant manticore. Sings-to-Trees put a bowl of water in with him and draped the towel in the corner. He went back out to the porch.

Frogsnoggler had waited. Sings-to-Trees picked up the bottle of iodine, turned around, and sighed.

The troll's eyes riveted on the bottle. Its mouth sagged in a parody of despair. "Grawh."

"Come on, you're a big troll," said Sings-to-Trees. This was something of an understatement—Frogsnoggler was probably close to two tons and stood nearly eight feet tall. "And I know you're brave. You stood there while that fox bit you and never a peep."

"Graww..."

The elf put his hands on his hips. Frogsnoggler cowered away, one arm over its eyes. Trembling, the troll held out its injured arm. Tears welled in dinner-plate sized eyes.

This was the standard trollish response to all medical treatment, and Sings-to-Trees knew full well Frogsnoggler would have done the same thing for removing a splinter or splinting a bone, but he was still torn between wry amusement and feeling a bit like an ogre.

In truth, it was probably nothing—trolls sustained worse every time they went after a billy goat—but still, foxes weren't known for their clean mouths. He brandished the iodine bottle and a clean rag.

The troll sniffled through the whole operation. Finally, Sings-to-Trees set the rag aside. "All done!"

Frogsnoggler inched its hand down from its eyes and gazed at him worriedly.

"Really, all done," said the elf, and patted the troll's shoulder. "And you were very brave. I'm proud of you."

A smile cracked the immense face. Frogsnoggler leapt up and cut an elephantine caper around Sings-to-Trees. "Grah! Grahgrahgrah!"

"Now, if that gets infected—if it turns red, or it starts to smell bad—I want you to come back here, okay?"

"Grah!"

"Then go on home before the sun fries you."

The troll nodded, reached out a hand, and patted Sings-to-Trees rather heavily on the shoulder.

"Oh—" In return, the elf patted the troll's knuckles, which had wiry black hair growing from them. "I'll probably release the fox in two or three days, if you want to come back and see him."

"Graah!" Frogsnoggler said happily, and turned and

scampered—insomuch as something the size of a team of oxen can scamper—into the woods.

Sings-to-Trees chuckled to himself. He did love trolls. They were so immensely good-hearted. He didn't know how they managed to be voracious predators—every time they saw a wounded animal, they brought it to him instead of eating it. This wasn't the first patient that had come to him in the arms of a troll.

(Once it had been a half-grown moose. The moose had been a fairly straightforward job—barbed wire wrapped around one leg—but treating the addled troll, who'd been kicked half-senseless had taken most of the night.)

He went back in and checked on the fox. It was resting now, still breathing more shallowly than he'd like, but sleeping all the same. There were herbs he needed, but his supply was running low. He really needed to go out to the bog meadow and pick some before the season turned completely and everything dried out.

And there, of course, went the rest of the afternoon.

He laughed a bit to himself as he picked up a basket. He should have known, of course—there was never any free time that wasn't filled immediately with a crisis—but he felt good anyway. Between the sleeping fox and the capering troll, his earlier glum mood had broken up. Maybe he *would* be doing this when he was old. Someone had to.

And if he needed a seeing-eye troll to help him around the farm, he suspected he only had to ask.

Stepping out onto the porch again, he glanced around for the trap. It wouldn't do to step on it, but he hadn't seen where Frogsnoggler had dropped it.

He got down the front steps and saw it. The troll, casually and without fanfare, had reduced the trap to fragments of twisted metal. Sings-to-Trees could not have duplicated the destruction without a hammer and possibly a forge.

The elf made a faint, thoughtful sound to himself and went off to gather herbs.

The farmhouse was very quiet.

It was too quiet.

Generally, when people say it's "too quiet," it's a prelude to a monster with a lot of teeth jumping out of the grass. In this case, however, since the only thing that could qualify as monsters with a lot of teeth were the goblins themselves, it was just plain too quiet.

The farmhouse was a small sod building—and that was odd, too, since there was a whole forest right there, and who builds out of sod when they have wood?—and the fences were the low dry-stone affairs that look cute and quirky and charming until you realize they're made of all the rocks that some poor farmer had to haul out of a field by hand.

There was wood, but not much. The timbers were in place only where nothing else would do. A few scattered tree stumps around the farm showed where they had probably come from.

It was a neatly kept yard, with a small henhouse and a pigpen. Around back, a low stable held three empty stalls.

It was very, very quiet.

"Perhaps they went into town. The horses aren't here."

"And took the pigs and chickens with them?" asked Murray skeptically.

A rising, rattling hum startled them all, until they realized that one of the trees dotting the property had cicadas in it. The insects buzzed their way up the register, and then fell silent.

It was still too quiet.

"Maybe it was market day? They took the pigs and chickens in to sell?"

"Every single one, Sarge?"

"Do you have a better explanation?"

Algol cleared his throat. "They must have looked pretty odd carrying all those chickens and walking. The wagon's still here."

They all looked at the wagon. It was distinctly wagon-like. The cicadas buzzed again.

"Check the henhouse."

They made their way around the farmhouse. Coming out of the woods, they had been moving like goblins on a raid—low to the ground, skulking, hiding behind things. It was beginning to seem silly in this deep, abandoned silence, but Nessilka hadn't lived this long by going into enemy territory and sauntering around in the open.

Besides, it was so quiet that it was almost comforting to crouch behind water barrels and old haystacks. It made you feel like you could hide from that terrible silence.

The last stretch to the henhouse had no cover for anyone over six inches tall. Crouched behind the compost bin, the three goblins eyed the distance. Nessilka gritted her teeth, squared her shoulders, and said, "Wait here."

She didn't run. Goblins know all about monsters—they're related, after all—and they know all about the rules. Like small children, they know the rules in their bones. If there was something out there, something cloaking itself in the silence, if she ran, it could run, too.

She *walked*, therefore, to the door of the henhouse, over earth packed hard and littered with old chicken droppings and bits of straw, while the skin between her shoulders and on the back of her neck crept and crawled and cringed.

Algol and Murray huddled together, shoulder to shoulder, biting their lips. The sergeant reached out, caught the wire door, and flung it open.

Sunlight lanced down through cracks in the ceiling and made pale spots on the straw. Old dust, old straw, old feathers. There were reasonably fresh droppings near the door, but no clucking greeted her, and there was no movement of nervous chickens along the walls.

She considered looking behind the door. She decided not to tempt fate.

She closed the door instead and walked back across the courtyard with a deliberately steady tread.

"Empty," she said in a low voice. "For a few days, probably."

Algol, without saying anything, crab-walked over to the pigpen and looked over the fence. The other two followed him.

"There's still a half bucket of slops here, Sarge," he said quietly.

"Well, that's not that weird—"

"Have you ever known pigs to leave *any* slops behind 'em?"

They stood around the slop bucket like three witches around a cauldron. It was indeed half-full. The sides of the bucket had crusted and dried, and there was mold growing in the bottom.

Algol dipped a finger in, pulled it out covered in gunk, and popped it in his mouth, rolling the tastes around like a gourmand.

"More than three days. Less than a week. Needs more salt."

They stood in silence, then, as one, looked at the farmhouse. Nessilka sighed.

"Okay, what are you guys thinking?"

"Plague, maybe?" said Algol.

Murray shook his head. "No bodies. And where'd the chickens go?"

"Maybe they buried the bodies and took the chickens."

"Doesn't explain the pig slop. And I haven't seen anything that could be grave markers."

"Maybe they left suddenly? Bandits?"

"No blood, and they wouldn't have taken live chickens. And it still doesn't explain the pig slop."

"Maybe bandits killed the pigs before they were done eating."

"No blood in the pen. And the place is in pretty good shape. Bandits would have wrecked the joint."

"Could they be hiding?" Algol jerked his chin at the farmhouse.

"With the pigs, and the chickens, and the mules or whatever ought to be in those empty stalls? It's not that big a house."

They all looked at the house in question again. Nessilka nodded.

"Okay, let's go in. Don't bother sneaking; let's just get this over with."

In a properly run universe, the door would have opened with one of those long creaks that go on forever, but it was hung on leather-strap hinges and swung open silently.

The interior was dark and quiet. Two chairs, one table, one bed. A thin film of dust lay over everything. The goblins looked toward the bed, which was unmade, but empty, and breathed a sigh of relief.

A plate of food lay on the table, with a fork next to it. There was a piece of elderly broccoli speared on the end of the fork. Mold fuzzed most of the other contents of the plate.

Algol stepped onto something that groaned, and they all jumped. He leapt back, revealing a square wooden trapdoor set in the floor.

"Root cellar, probably," said Nessilka. Her father had been a mountain goblin, and she had no fear of tunnels or holes, but she found she really, really didn't want to go down there.

Algol and Murray looked ready to bolt. She reminded

herself that it was just as alarming for them, and they were from hill and marsh and didn't even have the advantage of having tunnels in their blood.

"You two stay up here until I call."

The corporals visibly relaxed.

She grabbed the handle on the trapdoor, counted to three, and yanked it up.

Dust floated down from the opening, but that was all. A ladder led down into the earth.

Nessilka pulled her stub of candle from her kit and lit it. "Here goes nothing..."

She didn't know what she was expecting. No, that was a lie. She was *expecting* to find a couple of dead bodies, and possibly something gnawing on them. *Please, gods, let me be wrong. Please let it be empty...*

The gods were kind. The root cellar was barely large enough to turn around in, full of shelves that groaned under the weight of canned preserves. The floor was dirt, the walls were dirt, and somebody had tossed an old burlap sack on the ground to soak up spills. And that was all.

There were no bodies, unless somebody had canned them.

I really wish I hadn't thought that.

"Well, at least we won't starve. Murray!"

Murray's head appeared in the hole. "Yes, Sarge?"

"Have Algol stand guard, and help me lug these up. See if there's a blanket we can carry this stuff in."

There was a set of rough blankets on the bed, which were a welcome find all on their own. Murray rigged two slings with harness leather scavenged from the stable, and they filled them with jars of indeterminate preserves. Most of them seemed to be peaches, with some dark red things that might have been meat, tomatoes, plums, or oddly colored peaches thrown in for good measure.

Thus loaded, Murray and Nessilka did a quick sweep of the farmhouse. A frying pan and an iron pot were too good to pass up—Nessilka did not want to be making tea in Blanchett's helmet on a regular basis—along with a small sack of salt and a bigger sack of flour.

They emerged from the house, heavily laden and clanking as they walked. Despite the mysterious emptiness of the farm, discovering the food couldn't help but raise their spirits. This lasted for a good five seconds before Nessilka said, "Where's Algol?"

The two goblins looked around. "He was right out here . . ." Murray said.

"Algol!" hissed Nessilka. She didn't want to yell. She couldn't shake the feeling that yelling would bring something down on them. "Algol, where *are* you?"

The cicadas were the only answer.

"He can't have gone far," muttered Nessilka.

"Unless whatever got the farmers got him, too," said Murray glumly.

"Put a lid on it, Corporal."

Murray gave her the look that said, *You know I'm right, but it's okay. I understand you have to say that.* She hated that look. She just couldn't do anything about it because he usually *was* right, hang it all.

"We can't just leave without him," she said slowly, scanning the fields. "But I don't want to stay out here in plain sight, either . . ." Far across the fields, she could barely make out the town. It wasn't close enough to see any people, and they probably couldn't have seen the goblins either, but still, better safe than sorry.

Murray dug out his looky-tube-thing. Nessilka opened her mouth to say that she'd check behind the farmhouse, and then stopped. Splitting up did not seem like a good idea.

She fiddled with a strap on her sling.

"Sarge . . ."

"Did you find him?"

"No. But—Sarge—there's no smoke over at the town."

"It's pretty warm out. Why would there be smoke?"

"A town that size is going to have a blacksmith. Plus, there's a windmill over there, which means there's a miller, and where there's millers, there's usually a baker, except there isn't. And even when it's warm, people have to cook. But none of the chimneys are going at all. There's no smoke in the sky anywhere. And I don't see any horses or cows in the fields."

He raised the tube again and stopped. Nessilka pushed the tube gently back down. "Corporal," she said quietly, "let's not borrow trouble. Let's just find Algol and get out of here."

He wasn't behind the farmhouse. He wasn't in the chicken coop. Nessilka's nerves were fraying badly, and there was a cold stone in her gut. Murray kept yanking on his ponytail as if hoping to find Algol hiding somewhere inside it.

"Well," she said finally. "I suppose—"

"Sarge!"

Murray pointed. She whirled.

Across the fields, coming out of a drainage ditch, was a familiar tall gray-green figure.

Nessilka exhaled. It seemed to come from her toes. She stomped toward him, furious and relieved all at once.

"Corporal, what in the name of the great grim gods do you think you're—"

"Look, Sarge!" he cried, holding something over his head.

It was small. It was muddy. It wiggled.

It was a kitten.

Algol was covered in mud and grinning from ear to ear.

"Oh, for gods' sake . . ." said Nessilka, covering her eyes.

"I heard him mewing! He was stuck down in a pipe in the ditch, and I got him out. Can I keep 'im, Sarge? Can I? Please?"

"Corporal—" she began, and stopped because she didn't know what she was going to say after that. She should never have let him name the supply goat. Once you started naming goats, it was all downhill from there. She massaged the bridge of her nose and tried again. "Corporal, we're goblins. The scourge of the night! Stealers of children! Marauders of the dark! The terror of . . . well, fairly terrible anyway."

Algol looked at her blankly, petting the kitten.

"We aren't kitten people!"

Algol stared at her, still petting the kitten. It made a little *mrrp!* noise and butted its head against his big fingers. "But Sarge, he was *stuck*."

"We're behind enemy lines! We don't know how we're going to get back! And you want to adopt a kitten?"

Algol sniffed. The sergeant could see a traitorous moisture beginning under his eyes.

"We can't leave 'im," he said quietly. "He's the only thing alive out here. He'll die."

"Corporal—"

His lower lip wibbled.

"Oh, *fine*," she said, relenting. "If somebody eats it, don't come crying to me."

"Thank you, Sarge!" Algol thrust the kitten at her face. Nessilka recoiled. "Look, kitty! This is Sarge! She says I can keep you! Say hi!"

The stealer of children and marauder of the dark grudgingly reached up and petted the kitten. It licked her finger with a raspy little tongue. She grumbled. It purred.

"By rights I oughta have you thrown in the stockade, abandoning your post like that . . ." she muttered.

"We don't really have a stockade, Sarge," Murray pointed out.

"I oughta make him build one, then!"

Algol, besotted with his kitten, ignored this.

Nessilka threw her hands in the air. "Don't do it again, Corporal, or I'll bust you back down to private so fast . . ."

"I think I'll name him Wiggles. He looks like a Wiggles."

Nessilka knew when she was beaten. Wiggles perched on Algol's shoulder and purred the entire way back to camp.

THE TEDDY BEAR, by way of Blanchett, had nothing to report. The twins were asleep in a pile, looking like lumpy green kittens themselves. Gloober was exploring the inner reaches of his left ear. All appeared right with the world.

The returning goblins slung the preserves off their shoulders and set about making tea, in the pot this time. Blanchett was pleased to get his helmet back.

Nessilka had just taken the first sip—sweet, gritty, fairly revolting, exactly what she'd been looking for—when Weasel burst out of the bushes.

"S-S-SARGE!"

Aw, crud.

The little goblin was scarlet-faced, and her hair had come out of its tight tail. Sweat glued it across her cheeks. Her chest heaved.

"It-t-t's Th-th-th—"

"Calm down, kiddo." Nessilka knew it was the height of rudeness to finish sentences for somebody with a stutter, but this sounded like an emergency. "Something's happened to Thumper. Sit down, take a deep breath . . . okay, now tell me what it is."

"He's hu-hu-hurt! It's el-el-el—"

"Elves?"

Weasel nodded furiously.

"Did elves hurt him?"

She nodded, then shook her head, then threw her hands in the air. Nessilka interpreted this, correctly, as a sign of a tale too complex to be summed up in yes or no questions.

"Okay, guys, let's move. Take me where you last saw him, kiddo, and tell me on the way."

As near as Nessilka could piece together from the badly upset Weasel, she and Thumper had been doing fairly well. They'd flushed a bird, and Weasel had dropped it with her sling.

Then it started to go bad.

When they'd startled the bird, they had also startled a deer. The deer took off across a clearing, and Thumper, seeing a whole banquet on the hoof, took off after it.

The fact that a goblin couldn't possibly catch a deer on foot had apparently not occurred to him. The deer ran, he ran, they broke into a clearing in the woods, and then he put his foot in a hole and went down hard.

Weasel's first thought was that he'd broken a leg, but she didn't get close enough to see because the other occupant of the clearing had straightened up at that point.

It was an elf.

The elf had gone over to Thumper and crouched down, and Weasel didn't know what to do. Was he killing Thumper? Was Thumper killing him?

Minutes dragged by. If it had been anyone else, Nessilka would have wondered why they didn't attack, but she wouldn't have put Weasel up against an injured field mouse. Sure, a sling could kill somebody if you used it right, but she'd have laid odds the thought hadn't even occurred to the little goblin.

The elf stood up with a grunt. An unconscious Thumper was slung over his shoulder. There was blood on the goblin's head and a crude bandage. Bent nearly double, the elf made his way slowly across the clearing and into the woods.

At this point, Weasel proved her worth completely. She knew she couldn't track the elf once he was gone, and she was pretty sure no one else in the Nineteenth could either. Quick and quiet as her namesake, she followed.

The elf had gone for nearly a mile, stopping occasionally to rest and set Thumper down. Weasel noted that the elf was being surprisingly gentle with his captive and that he checked bandage, pulse, and pupils at every stop. It wasn't the behavior she'd expect from elves, but then, she'd never seen one anywhere but the other end of a sword before.

At last, the elf emerged into a large meadow, bright with wildflowers and dotted with bumblebees. On the far side, a large cabin rose under the trees, surrounded by a neat garden and a ramshackle barn.

The elf set Thumper down and went to the barn. As soon as he vanished, Weasel darted out and shook Thumper's shoulder, but the big goblin was out like a light. His forehead was sporting an enormous lump. Either the elf had clobbered him a good one, or he'd smacked his head on a rock when he'd fallen in the meadow.

The elf re-emerged from the barn, pushing a wheelbarrow. Weasel dropped low and scurried back to the tree line. As she watched, the elf set Thumper into the wheelbarrow and took him up to the cabin.

Weasel had watched only until Thumper vanished inside the cabin, and then had turned and run like a rabbit back to the Nineteenth.

It took all the way back to the clearing to get this story out of the agitated Weasel, and even then, seeing the scene helped solidify the details.

It was a very pastoral clearing, one of those that look lovely and lush and green and turn out to be sopping wet marsh under the plants. Sweet flag irises poked up proudly over the long grass. Nessilka went over the ground carefully and found the hole. It had a large goblin footprint in the mud at the bottom of it. A handprint skidded off to one side.

There was a rock the size of a pig directly in front of it, with blood on it.

"Hmm." Murray crouched down and looked. "I'd say he stepped, fell, tried to catch himself, his hand slipped, and he whacked his head. And then the elf came up here." He pointed to a line of heavy boot prints.

"Believe it or not, I could probably have figured all that out on my own," said Nessilka a bit dryly.

"Sorry, Sarge."

"It does mean that the elf probably didn't hit him. Which may mean he's not violently opposed to all goblins. It's possible we'll be able to get Thumper back peacefully."

"And if we can't?"

Nessilka stood up and looked around at the other seven goblins. The teddy bear and Wiggles the kitten watched from atop their respective owner's heads. They did not look very warlike, but they were what she had.

"Then," she said, "we'll get him back by any means necessary."

The elf was out in his garden, with his back to them. As the goblins approached, he straightened, rubbing his back and grimacing. Nessilka couldn't blame him—lugging someone Thumper's size over his shoulder must have been agony.

Nessilka figured stealth wasn't exactly called for here. She cleared her throat.

He turned around.

Eight goblins in a tight knot, bristling with swords, clubs, and boards with nails in them, faced him.

The elf was about six feet tall and lanky, with white hair in a loose braid and quizzical eyebrows.

His clothes were odd. Elves usually looked immaculate. It was how you could tell they were elves. You could cut an elf's leg off, and he would contrive to make it look as if two legs were unfashionable. Elves were just like that. It was one of their more annoying traits.

This one wore a loose shirt that had been washed so many times the sleeves had shrunk, revealing bony wrists, and pants with carefully patched knees. He had the usual elven cheekbones, but they were smudged with dirt. He was practically scruffy.

He didn't look scared. He didn't look angry. He didn't even look very surprised—probably he'd known that where there was one goblin, more would be coming—but he did look a little bemused.

His almond-shaped eyes traveled over the goblins, not missing either Wiggles or the teddy bear.

"Say something!" hissed Nessilka, elbowing Murray in the ribs.

"What? Why me?"

"You speak Elvish! Say something useful!"

"I—but—"

"Do it!"

Murray gulped, faced the elf, and stammered out a long phrase in Elvish, like a child repeating a speech it has learned by heart.

The elf's eyebrows climbed until they nearly touched his hairline. He said something brief and jerked a thumb to the left.

Murray nodded weakly.

"What did you say?" Nessilka demanded.

"I asked him where the bathroom was."

"*What? Why?*"

"It's the only sentence I know! I think he said it was around back!"

"I thought you spoke Elvish!"

"Not very well!"

Nessilka ground the heel of her hand into her forehead.

When she looked up, the elf was watching her. She was expecting to find an expression of contempt or hatred or *something*, but he met her eyes with unexpected camaraderie, like the only other babysitter in a room full of children. *How odd that our lives should bring us to this point*, that look said.

Despite herself, Nessilka warmed to that look.

Okay. Can't speak Elvish. I know a fair bit of Human, but there's no telling if the humans here speak the same as the ones where we're from . . .

The elf cleared his throat. "Can you understand me?" he asked, in fair, if oddly accented Glibber.

The Nineteenth stared at him. Nessilka exhaled. "Oh, thank the great grim gods," she said. "You speak a civilized language."

He smiled a little at that. "It has been many years. But if you speak slowly, I think I can keep up. Now, you are probably here to see your friend, yes?"

They all nodded.

"Please follow me."

14

The inside of the house was one large room with high rafters and a kitchen, a fireplace, and a bed. The kitchen contained a very long wooden table, the fireplace contained a broad hearth with a raccoon sleeping on it, and the bed contained Thumper.

"Thumper!" The Nineteenth crowded around the bed. Thumper cracked one eye, groaned, and closed it again.

"Report, Private!" snapped Nessilka.

"... no."

"No?"

"... no, *Sarge*," muttered Thumper.

She grinned hugely with relief. "I knew no rock could make that big a dent in your skull. Rest, you big idiot."

"... where'm I ... ?"

"You're—ah—safe." She looked up at the elf, who nodded. "Get some rest."

"... can't march ..."

"We're not gonna leave you, Thumper. No goblin left behind and all that. Relax."

It was not like Thumper to smile, but his scowl had a relieved quality as he sank back into sleep.

THE ELF'S NAME was Sings-to-Trees, and he liked animals.

This was something of an understatement.

Many people like animals in the abstract. Sings-to-Trees liked them the way saints like lepers. He lived with them, he treated them, he patched them up and fed them and sent them on their way. In return, they kicked him and bled on him and oozed on him and had offspring in the middle of his bed, which was admittedly something that saints have rarely had to worry about from the lepers.

"Your friend'll be fine," he told Nessilka. "It's nice having a patient who can actually answer questions. And before you worry"—he held up a hand—"I know there's a war on, but it's about fifty miles thataway. Your friend is hurt, and this isn't the front, so I'm not planning on turning you in. But you sure are a long way from home."

Nessilka nodded glumly. "Tell me about it. We didn't plan to be here. There was a wizard, and you know how it goes . . ."

He nodded. "I doubt anybody's going to find you. Other elves don't come by here much. A little too much nature for them, I think."

"I thought all elves . . . y'know . . . were into nature . . ." said Nessilka, with a vague hand gesture that could have indicated either into-nature-ness or raving insanity.

Sings-to-Trees snorted. "Sure. Pretty nature. Unicorns, griffins, hummingbirds, sylphs, those little dragon-butterfly things . . . the animals that don't smell bad and look pretty. But you get an egg-bound cockatrice that needs its cloacal vents oiled three times a day for a week, and suddenly everybody has pressing engagements elsewhere."

("What's a cloacal vent?" Mishkin asked Algol, who told him. Both twins turned a little gray and gazed at Sings-to-Trees with awed disgust.)

"And just try to get them to patch up a troll. Trolls are *wonderful*." He was pacing now. Nessilka got the impression that this was a rant he'd been working on for a long time, and he didn't often get a new audience. "They'd let you saw off their head without flinching. I *love* trolls. And they keep you in all the goat meat you can eat, too. But if one gets lost and goes wandering through some elf's backyard, are they understanding? Noooo, it's all 'Call out the guards, there's a rogue troll on the loose!' Bah! Trolls are like *kittens*." He stabbed a finger in the direction of Wiggles for emphasis, then paused.

"Which reminds me, let me get you some food for that little guy."

"So how did you learn to speak Glibber at all?" asked Murray, while Sings-to-Trees prepared a saucer of mince for the kitten and Murray made tea. All eight of the uninjured goblins had crowded around the long table in the kitchen. The wood was scarred from countless claws, and the edges had a distinctly gnawed look.

"There used to be a lot of goblins here. Some were my friends. I used to treat their pigs." He smiled. "Sometimes I'd treat them, too—I don't know if the state of goblin medicine has advanced much in the last hundred years—"

"No, it's still pretty much 'amputate at the neck,'" said Murray.

The elf nodded. "I was sorry when the tribe left. They were company, anyway. Most elves don't come out this far. The humans aren't bad, really. I help their animals sometimes. Somebody comes up from the town every couple of days with cheese or bread or some such."

Algol, Murray, and Nessilka slid glances at each other, then quickly away. Murray looked at the ceiling, and Algol looked at the floor. Nessilka ran a finger through a groove on the side of the table, which seemed to be a tooth mark from something with teeth the size of her thumb.

"Has anyone come up in the last few days?" she asked quietly.

The elf's forehead twisted. "There was bread and cheese . . . no, that was a while ago. Now that you mention it, no. Nobody's dropped off food for almost a week."

Nessilka nodded slowly. "We were just at the village. Well, at a farmhouse. There's nobody there."

"You mean they left?"

"No . . . I mean, there's nobody there. The wagon's there, but no people. No animals. A meal left in mid-bite." She shook her head. "We didn't check the village, obviously, but we didn't see anyone."

The elf shook his head. "That's odd. That's really worrisome. Perhaps I should go look."

Nessilka didn't want to go anywhere near that farmhouse again, but—well—he *had* fixed Thumper, and he did speak their language, and he wasn't turning them in. It would probably be better if he didn't get a chance to go off alone and have second thoughts about that last bit, come to think of it.

"We'll go with you, in the morning," said Nessilka. Murray made a faint noise of protest, and she silenced him with a glare. "We can at least show you where the abandoned farm was."

"Thank you. You're more than welcome to stay here for the night—your friend's going to be on his back for at least three days, even as hard as goblin heads are. I want him in here, so I can check on him every few hours, but if you all don't mind sleeping in the barn . . ."

"With real straw?" asked Mishkin.

"And a real roof?" asked Mushkin.

"All the straw and roof you want."

The twins cheered.

"We should probably get dinner started, too."

Nessilka raised her eyebrows. "Are you sure you want to feed all eight of us? You're helping Thumper already. I don't want to eat you out of house and home."

Sings-to-Trees laughed in what he probably thought was a maniacal fashion, but there was something so inherently harmless about him that it looked more like he was practicing a peculiar bird call. "Are you kidding? Finally, an excuse to get rid of all of that zucchini! I planted two plants this year, and now not even the trolls will come by for fear I'll throw zucchini bread at them." He started for the door.

"Okay, then . . . Mishkin, Mushkin, go help the nice man with his zucchini. Algol, take Weasel and see to moving our stuff into the barn. Try to make as little mess as possible; we're guests. Gloober, if you stick your finger any farther in your ear, you'll go deaf, and I'll have to learn sign language so I can say, 'I told you so.' Go help with the zucchini. Try not to put one in your ear."

Having thus disposed of the troops, Murray, Blanchett, and Nessilka were left sitting alone at the long wooden table. Nessilka swirled the dregs of her tea around her mug.

"What do you think?" she asked Murray.

"I think that it's highly unlikely he and Algol were separated at birth, but I still wonder."

"Nah, I've met Algol's mother. Lovely woman, but goblin to the bone. Do you think we can trust him?"

Murray pulled on his ponytail. "We don't have much choice until Thumper gets better, do we? I don't know. If you're asking whether I think he's keeping us here until he can call in the elves, I don't think so. He really doesn't seem like the type."

"The bear trusts him," put in Blanchett.

Point in his favor, thought Nessilka. *The bear is usually a pretty good judge of character. And that I'm even thinking that is probably a sign that I need my head examined.*

SINGS-TO-TREES STRAIGHTENED UP and watched the goblins picking zucchini. The twins were an indeterminate shade of gray-brown, and their lumpy, dirt-streaked skin blended surprisingly well with the earth. If they hadn't been cheerfully finishing each other's sentences, he would have had a hard time spotting them.

He had been startled by the goblin—Thumper—running

across the field, but once the poor fellow had hit his head, there wasn't much help for it but to take him home. He'd known the others were going to show up, of course. You never got just one goblin. The surprising thing was that there were any here at all, what with the war.

Sings-to-Trees had always rather liked goblins. They reminded him of tiny trolls—ferocious looking, often foul, but generally without malice. He had no particular opinion about the war, except that it was probably a shame. In his experience, people were usually people, even the ones who were four feet tall and lumpy, and if you treated them well, they mostly returned the favor.

He was quite sure the sergeant—the rather imposing female goblin with the bun and the put-upon expression—didn't quite trust him, but in her position, he wouldn't have trusted him either.

Despite all warnings to the contrary, the one named Gloober was trying to insert a zucchini up his nose. Sings-to-Trees sighed and went to rescue his vegetables from a fate worse than death.

THE GOBLINS APPROVED of the zucchini, in goblin fashion. They sat around the table on barrels, crates, and anything else that would hold them, complaining happily.

"This is terrible!"

"Worst zucchini I've ever seen! Looks like baked dog turds!"

"And they're gritty! Did you even wash them?"

"What's with this bread? I could use it to fix my boots!"

"I think this butter's about to turn."

The Nineteenth polished off three bowls apiece, five loaves of zucchini bread, and Mishkin and Mushkin were licking the casserole dish clean. Nessilka opened her mouth to explain the cultural differences to the elf and that he was actually receiving a compliment, only to find him standing behind Blanchett's chair and beaming. Apparently he really did know goblins.

"Okay, troops, take the man's bowls out to the pump and wash 'em. And don't half-ass it, either. I want those clean enough to see my reflection! Murray, go supervise."

Murray saluted idly and began herding the goblins out of the house. Blanchett started to rise, and Nessilka caught his shoulder. "Not you, Blanchett. I want to see if we can do anything about your ankle."

"Aww, Sarge . . ."

Sings-to-Trees knelt on the floor and caught Blanchett's foot in one hand. Nessilka revised her opinion of the elf's courage upward. She'd have used tongs.

"Does this hurt? Does this? How about this?"

After a few moments of prodding, he dropped the foot and vanished into the kitchen, absently wiping his hands on his tunic. "Just a moment . . ."

After a minute, Nessilka got up and began wandering restlessly through the house, listening to the bang of crockery from the next room.

It was a decent house. It didn't look like the kind of place an enemy would live. There were no swords crossed on the walls or severed goblin heads mounted over the fireplace. The house was a little too clean and airy for a goblin, but it had a comfortable, lived-in look, with battered furniture and faded rugs.

There was a young raccoon in the hutch by the fire. She hooked a finger through the mesh, and it licked her hand.

Even the raccoons were friendly.

Nessilka felt that she ought to keep her guard up because she was in enemy territory, damn it, in the very home of the foe, but it was hard when she was stuffed on the foe's zucchini bread and the foe's baby raccoon was slurping at her fingers.

Sings-to-Trees emerged from the kitchen, arms full of pottery. Steam wreathed his face and plastered lank blond hair to his forehead.

"Your ankle'll be fine," he told the goblin, slathering some kind of herbal plaster on it. It made Blanchett smell very strongly of mustard, which was something of an improvement over smelling very strongly of goblin. "Now drink this."

Blanchett eyed the mug of murky brown herbs warily. "How do I know you're not trying to poison me?"

Sings-to-Trees sighed and dipped a finger into the mug, then slurped the liquid off it. "There. Happy?"

"Well, now you've put your finger in it!"

Nessilka figured it was time to intervene. "Private, I know for a fact you haven't washed your hands since the war started. You have no business complaining about anybody else's fingers. Drink the nice gunk already."

Blanchett rolled his eyes upward, possibly appealing to the authority of his teddy bear. After a moment, he grimaced. "He says to drink it."

"Listen to the bear. The bear is smart. Also, that's an order."

With a much-put-upon expression, Blanchett drained the mug.

"Huh. Tastes like rat squeezins with too much honey." He considered. "Can I get the recipe?"

"Get outta here," muttered Nessilka, aiming a swat in his general direction. Blanchett dodged with surprising agility and hobbled out in good humor.

"Thanks," she said to Sings-to-Trees.

The elf waved dismissively. "He didn't try to bite, kick, or gore. He's already an improvement over most of my patients."

She grinned. She couldn't help it.

He passed her another mug of tea. "It might taste like rat squeezins, mind you. Whatever a rat squeezin is."

She rolled the liquid around on her tongue. "You're probably happier not knowing. Anyway, tastes like mud and rancid sticks to me."

He raised an eyebrow.

"That means it's good."

He nodded. "I remember. Took me awhile to get used to the

goblin . . . err . . . courtesies." He gestured with his own mug.

"Really, thank you," she said. "It's damn decent of you, feeding us and letting us stay here for a few days. We were—well, we're not really cut out for the woods."

"I'm glad to help." Sings-to-Trees stared into his own mug, possibly looking for the elusive rat squeezins. "Anyway, if the town really is deserted, I'd be glad of company."

"Thanks for that, too," Nessilka said.

"Hmm? For what?"

"For not immediately assuming that we'd done something to the people in the village. You didn't even ask. That . . . I appreciate that."

He smiled faintly. "I've known too many goblins. They're . . . crude, and sometimes they're a bit wicked, but I've never known them to be vicious. It surprised me to hear there was even a goblin war."

"We had to do something!" she bristled.

He nodded. The silence stretched out while he ran a finger over the tabletop. "For what it's worth, I'm sorry your people were driven to that. I wish there had been another way."

"Heh!" Her laugh startled them both. "That's the first time anybody's apologized."

Odd little words, "I'm sorry." Nessilka found that she didn't feel any better about the war, but she did feel a bit better about Sings-to-Trees.

"So—you said there was magic? Some poor wizard sent you?"

Nessilka nodded. "I think he was trying to escape the battle, but we all came with him. It knocked him out cold, anyway."

Sings-to-Trees gave her a worried look. "What did you do with him?"

It was embarrassing, but she suddenly found herself afraid that she might disappoint the elf, which made her feel defensive. "There wasn't much we could do," she snapped. "We couldn't very well take him with us, and when a bunch of goblins show up at a human town with a human body, people tend to shoot first and not bother with the question bit at all!"

He was silent. Nessilka sighed. She had to stop snapping at him. He took it all as patiently as he probably took having manticores vomit on him, but it wasn't fair. He was one elf. She couldn't make him stand for every elf that had ever been on the other end of a sword from her.

"Sorry. I feel guilty, and it's making me cross. We put a blanket over him, and Algol got some water into him. I didn't know what else we could do."

The elf nodded. "Honestly, I don't know what else you could have done. Water and a blanket was a good thing. I could wish for a fire and food in him, but wizards . . . well, if one woke up to a goblin troop, it could go very badly. Poor guy."

He pondered. "I can send a pigeon to the rangers and tell them to keep an eye out for a shocky wizard in that part of the woods." He paused. "If you'd like to read it first—I wasn't going to tell them about you, but I understand—"

Nessilka shrugged. "I can't read Elvish, and it'd look awfully odd if you sent them a note in Glibber, wouldn't it?"

"There's that." Sings-to-Trees looked into his mug, seemed surprised to find it empty, and began digging in a tin for more tea. "I wonder why the wizard picked that as an escape route, though," the elf mused. "They don't do well with surprises, most of them. I'd think one would want to go to a safe place, familiar surroundings. The middle of a forest under elven protection seems a little strange."

"Maybe he was from around here," said Nessilka, who'd been wondering something similar herself. "The humans from the town can go into the forest, right? As long as they don't cut the trees or overhunt?"

Sings-to-Trees nodded. "There are fairly strict rules and quotas, and the rangers check up on those, but generally we find that as long as they know what they can and can't do—

and that there'll be repercussions if they break the rules—the humans are pretty reliable."

Nessilka sighed. "Maybe that was our problem. We didn't make any rules; we just left."

Sings-to-Trees shrugged. "It might not have helped. The goblin tribes go everywhere, but they're usually pretty thin on the ground. You would have had a hard time enforcing the rules. Whereas elves—well—"

"You're tall and impressive looking, and you can put an arrow into a squirrel's eye from a hundred paces," said Nessilka.

"There's that, yeah. We had charisma and numbers and mayhem. All you had were pigs and enthusiasm. It's not your fault."

She called up the Goblin Army in her mind's eye and had to laugh. *Pigs and enthusiasm* described it pretty well.

The silence that stretched out was companionable. Dusk had finished with the trees and was starting to work across the yard. Crickets chirped, and a few fireflies telegraphed their attractiveness to the world.

She gathered the mug up to head back inside. "I should probably go make sure they haven't broken all your plates."

The elf shrugged and followed. "I've learned not to get too attached to plates. Here—take a lantern if you're headed to the barn for the night."

She glanced over at Thumper, still asleep. Sleeping on a head wound worried her. She hoped the elf knew what he was doing.

"I'll wake him every few hours. That's part of why I want him where I can keep an eye on him."

"Ah. Thank you." She grinned, showing blunt tusks. "I seem to keep thanking you."

Sings-to-Trees grinned back. "So few of my patients can. It's a nice change of pace."

Nessilka took the lantern down to the barn, where Algol and Murray were conscientiously overseeing the washing, and found, against all odds, that she was whistling.

It was still the small hours of the morning. The barn was smothered in shadow and in the rather thick smell of goblin digestion.

Someone was shaking her shoulder. Sergeant Nessilka opened one eye, saw The Enemy standing over her, and threw herself sideways before it could bring the lantern crashing down on her head. She snatched up her club and lifted it, eyes glittering in the orange light.

"Err," said Sings-to-Trees.

"Oh. Oh . . . *right*."

She straightened up and climbed out of the straw. "Sorry. Old habits . . ."

"I quite understand." He stood back politely while she roused Blanchett, Algol, and Murray. "Out of curiosity, are you often woken up that way?"

"Once. Night attack." The barn was warm, but the air coming through the door was cool and damp. She shrugged into her armor. "I broke his kneecaps."

"Ah."

"With my forehead."

"Goodness."

They left the rest of the Nineteenth behind, a symphony of snoring and gas in the dark barn. It was going to smell like a feedlot in there by dawn. Sings-to-Trees didn't seem particularly bothered by the idea.

They gathered in the kitchen. He handed around slices of toast and mugs of hot tea, which the goblins fell on gratefully. Murray wrapped his long fingers around the mug and inhaled the steam, his eyelids still at half-mast.

"Now," said Sings-to-Trees, checking through the contents of a pack. "You said there were no people and no livestock there. Did you notice anything that was there that shouldn't have been?"

"There was Wiggles," said Algol, patting the kitten, who was asleep on his lap. "But he was stuck in a drainpipe, so he probably doesn't count."

"Anything else?"

The goblins looked at each other helplessly and shrugged.

"We're not exactly experts on human farmhouses," said Murray. "We tend to see them rather ... err ... briefly. And we usually have something else on our mind at the time."

The elf nodded. "Well, I didn't expect anything, but I figured I'd ask. Everyone done with their breakfast?"

More nods. The Nineteenth was not big on conversation before noon.

"Guess we should get going, then."

Nessilka nodded. "Blanchett—can you walk? I wouldn't ask, but I want Algol in charge here, and I'd rather have you along with us." (This was almost true. Nessilka actually wanted the teddy bear, who seemed to have a good head on its stuffed shoulders.)

Blanchett tested the ankle. "Much better," he said. "The gunk helped. Shouldn't be a problem."

"You let me know if it is." She nodded to Algol. "You're in charge, Corporal. If anything happens ... err ..."

She realized that she had absolutely nothing to say to fill that gap, so she stopped.

"Will do, Sarge. Here, pet Wiggles for luck."

"Scourge of the night, Corporal."

"But he likes you!"

Nessilka relented and petted the kitten. She probably needed all the luck she could get.

Algol saluted. Nessilka saluted back. Sings-to-Trees watched them with an unreadable expression.

She wondered if he'd sent the pigeon to the rangers, and how he explained where he'd heard about a strange wizard.

They set out.

It was still twilight under the trees. They left dark green tracks in grass turned silver with dew, even Sings-to-Trees. Nessilka was sneakingly pleased by this. There were stories that elves could walk soundlessly and without a trace. It was nice to see that this one didn't.

Fleabane the coyote kept pace with them for a few minutes before peeling off on some canine errand of his own.

The forest got deeper and darker, even as the sun came up, so the net result was that the quality of light didn't change much. The ground stopped being grass and started being moss and then stopped being moss and became nothing but slick wet leaves. Everybody skidded a little on those, even the elf. And when you were that tall, whippy little branches tended to hit you in the face a lot more than when you were short.

It occurred to Nessilka that possibly the tales of elven slyness were much exaggerated... or possibly Sings-to-Trees was just a real klutz.

Except for the fact that they moved much more quietly and didn't fall into any poison ivy—and one of them was extremely tall—it wasn't much different than marching through the woods had been a day earlier.

And then Nessilka heard something.

It sounded like someone talking, but it wasn't in a language she recognized—or was it? She could almost make out the words. It had to be nearby; she could almost hear it all—was that one voice or two? What were they saying? The cadences were definitely speech, it wasn't an animal noise or a bird song, and if she could just get a little bit closer—

It occurred to her, somewhat later, that she was hurrying through the woods now, trying to make out the words. She could hear the footfalls of the others behind her. Undoubtedly they could hear it, too, but nobody was saying anything for fear of drowning out the words. What were they saying? She had to get a little bit closer, just a little bit, and she was sure she'd be able to make it out—

She was annoyed to find that her panting was making it harder to hear the voice. Was she panting? Yes, she'd been running, she was still running, but now she'd have to get even closer because she was wheezing like a blown horse, and Blanchett was saying, "Sarge? Sarge, what is it? Sarge?" and that was maddening because he was drowning out the voice—couldn't he *hear* it?

If she could only get close enough to make out what it was saying!

Sings-to-Trees could hear it, she was sure, because he was out in front of her now. The path had gotten very narrow, through steep dirt cliffs cut by tree roots, and it would have annoyed her that the elf was blocking her path, except that he was moving fast enough that she was having a hard time keeping up. Could he hear the voice? At least he panted more quietly than Murray, who was also wheezing, and Blanchett had fallen back—probably he couldn't keep up, with his hurt ankle, and the sounds of "Sarge?" were fading behind them, and that was good because it wasn't drowning out the voice any more—

A skeletal stag landed in the path directly in front of them with a warning clatter of bone. It sounded like the mother of all rattlesnakes. Sings-to-Trees stopped, and Nessilka let out a cry of frustration, and Murray plowed into the back of her.

They sorted themselves out wordlessly, practically dancing in place. "We have to get past it," said Murray.

"I know that," said Sings-to-Trees, "but it doesn't seem to want to let us!"

The stag lowered its magnificent white rack.

"We could backtrack," said Nessilka wretchedly. Backtracking would take them away from the voice and the conversation she was almost—*almost*—about to understand.

"No!" said Murray. He wiggled past Nessilka and made a short charge at the deer, perhaps hoping to bluff it.

The stag was apparently not inclined to bluff. It swung its head sideways, and white bone cracked against Murray's chest, knocking him down.

"Murray—"

Murray rolled over and began crawling determinedly forward. Could he get between the stag's feet? Nessilka cursed the fact that there wasn't room for two of them.

Sings-to-Trees's face twisted. "I don't want to hurt you," he pleaded with the stag. "I really, *really* don't. I helped your mate! Please, just let us pass!"

Another rattlesnake clatter. The stag danced in place, feet falling perilously close to Murray's head.

There was a second warning rattle. Nessilka looked over her shoulder and saw a bone doe standing there, watching them with empty eye sockets.

The voice continued to talk, a conversation that was probably about nothing, but it might be something *fascinating*, and anyway, she'd know in a minute if she could just get a little bit closer—

And then it stopped.

Sings-to-Trees, who had been about to charge the deer, completely bare-handed, stopped with an expression of horror on his face and looked down at his hands. "Oh," he said. "Oh. Oh, *no* . . ."

Murray said, "What in the name of the dead orc gods am I *doing*?"

Nessilka, seeing bone deer hooves like lances around the head of her second-in-command, reached down and grabbed him by the ankles. She hauled. Murray was very heavy, but female goblins tended to be strong all out of proportion to their size. He left long furrows in the mud behind him.

The bone deer stamped a hoof and nodded to Sings-to-Trees. Then it turned and reached the top of the narrow defile in a single leap. There was a second clack of bone, and the skeletal doe followed.

"She's still a bit short on the front foot," said Sings-to-Trees vaguely. "I hope it's healing. She shouldn't be making jumps like that. Oh gods, I was going to attack that poor creature!" He put his face in his hands.

"I suspect that poor creature would have torn you to shreds," said Nessilka drily. "Murray, how's your ribs?"

"Sore," said Murray. "It hit me, didn't it? I don't think it wanted to hurt me, though, whatever it was. No holes." He slid a finger under his leather breastplate and winced. "Nothing broken. Gonna have some fantastic bruises to show the recruits."

"It was a cervidian," said Sings-to-Trees. "They're attracted to magic. I saw it the other day—I can't believe I wanted to hurt it—"

Nessilka thumped him on the shoulder, which was the highest point she could reach. "Get over it, soldier," she snapped, forgetting he wasn't one of *her* soldiers. "You didn't, and that's the important thing. The most important thing, though, is *what the hell was wrong with us?*"

They all stared at each other.

"I heard a voice," said Murray uncertainly.

"So did I."

"I couldn't hear what it was saying," said Nessilka. "I almost could, but I thought if I could just get closer—"

"It had to be right around here, didn't it?" Sings-to-Trees peered around the woods, puzzled. "I mean, we were really close to it . . . weren't we?"

"I don't think we were," said Murray slowly. "We've been running, haven't we? Blanchett couldn't keep up . . ."

"Oh gods, Blanchett!" Nessilka spun around. "We have to go get him!"

"He'll be fine," said Murray. "The bear'll take care of him."

Sings-to-Trees looked at them as if they were insane, which they probably were, but Nessilka did feel a bit better. "How long were we running?"

None of them knew.

"At least a mile, I think," said Murray. "It's hard to tell because it's cold out and the terrain's twisty, but I don't think I usually get this sweaty over anything less."

"We can't have been that close to the conversation for a whole mile," said Sings-to-Trees.

Nessilka had already come to that conclusion and a couple of others she didn't like at all.

Murray tugged on his ponytail. "It was magic, Sarge. Had to be."

"A voice that makes you want to get closer to it . . . That could explain why the farms were empty. They all left to get closer to the voice." Nessilka chewed on her lower lip. "Maybe it worked on the animals, too."

Sings-to-Trees looked around. "I don't hear any birds," he said. "But that could just as easily be the cervidian. It got real quiet around my farm when they showed up. I think they're just too uncanny."

"Well." Nessilka rubbed the back of her neck. "Options?"

"Find the source," said Murray immediately.

"Find out what happened to the farmers," said Sings-to-Trees.

Nessilka sighed. "Normally, I'd say we should go back and report this, but I don't know who we'd report it to."

"I could send a pigeon to the rangers," said Sings-to-Trees.

"How long would that take?"

"Um. It depends. A few hours at least. Probably more. I didn't actually send the other one yet—it's dark, they won't fly, so I was going to wait until we get back. Although I'm surprised they're not investigating already, frankly—nothing this big should be able to go down without them noticing."

"Unless they sent somebody to investigate and the voice got them too," said Murray. Sings-to-Trees winced.

"Okay," said Nessilka. She mostly wanted to run away screaming, but she was in command, and Sings-to-Trees was a civilian and thus should probably be protected as much as possible. And he didn't seem to be much good at sneaking.

Also, there was the small problem of the village being between them and Goblinhome, and the grim gods only knew how far the range on that magic extended.

"Here's what we'll do. We find Blanchett, first. Then Sings-to-Trees goes back to the farm, and we'll scout the village."

"We should wear earplugs," volunteered Murray. "I can rig something up. I don't know how well they'll work, but if it really is a sound, we should be able to block it."

Nessilka was getting ready for the inevitable argument—Sings-to-Trees looked like he was about to argue—when there was a very welcome interruption.

"Sarge? Sarge!"

"Blanchett!" She turned and waved. A familiar teddy bear, atop an equally familiar helm, appeared over the top of the low cliff edging the road.

"There you are, Sarge! Didn't know why we were running, but the bear said you were somewhere around here . . ."

"Can you get down here?"

"Sure, give me a minute . . ." The helm disappeared.

"And while we're asking questions . . ." said Nessilka slowly, "why wasn't Blanchett affected?"

"Maybe the bear's immune," said Murray. And then, when Nessilka stared at him, "Have you got a better answer, Sarge?"

She didn't. For any of it, apparently. "All right," she said. "Make up your earplugs. I want to move out as soon as he gets here."

Sings-to-Trees did argue, but it seemed to Nessilka that it was more a matter of form. The encounter with the cervidian had shaken him badly, and what he really wanted was to get home and send a pigeon to the rangers as quickly as possible.

"You don't have to go," he said. "We could all go back. We'll let the rangers handle it."

The notion that someone higher up the chain of command would be more able to handle *anything* was so foreign to Nessilka that she couldn't really get her head around it. Could elves really be that different?

Naaaah. Elves were elves, but the military was the military. There was something immutable about it. Orcs were pretty different from goblins, too, but their military worked almost the exact same way, except that at the higher levels you were answerable to the priesthood, and nobody ever said anything nice about orcish gods.

"We'll investigate," said Nessilka. "Whatever this is, it's between us and our way home."

Sings-to-Trees sighed. "I'll come as far as the tree line, then," he said. "I promise I won't go after you, but if you get hurt, I'm . . . well, a veterinarian, but I've worked on goblins before."

Nessilka wavered.

"And if this is affecting animals too—" The elf wrung his hands.

She sighed. "Fine, fine. But you don't come after us. If something goes bad and we're not back by nightfall, you go back to the farm and you tell Algol what's happened."

And gods above, don't let Algol get a case of the heroics . . .

"I promise," said Sings-to-Trees. She eyed him warily, but he was a civilian—and another species—and she probably didn't have the authority to order him back to his farm.

Also, it was hard to assume authority when you only came up to the bottom of somebody's ribcage.

Blanchett scrambled down to them before long, covered in leaf mold and mud but none the worse for wear. (Actually, the mud improved his odor significantly.) Sings-to-Trees checked his ankle again and pronounced it acceptable.

"Tell me," said Murray, assembling earplugs out of moss and half an old candle, "did you hear the weird voice from earlier?"

Blanchett pushed a finger under his helmet to scratch. "I guess, yeah. Some kind of mumbling, wasn't it?"

"And you didn't feel any compulsion to go chase after it?"

Blanchett looked puzzled. "A what?"

"A comp—an overwhelming urge. You know?"

"Err. No?"

Murray gave it up as a bad job.

He finished the earplugs and handed them around. "This won't block all the sound. I don't have the equipment. But if you start to hear something, if you hum or sing, that should drown it out."

"Can I sing 'The Bird In The Bush'?" asked Blanchett hopefully.

Nessilka had a brief image of exactly how absurd the three of them would look trying to sneak up on the enemy while singing dirty drinking songs, and wondered if it would be any better if they were singing martial tunes or just humming really loudly. "Sing whatever you like, Blanchett."

"I'm not sure if they'll work even then," Murray said. "It might not be a real sound, you understand? If it's magic, it could be something in our heads as easily as anything else."

"We'll have to hope, then," said Nessilka. "Blanchett, this is a direct order. If you hear the weird mumbling again, and Murray and I start running toward it—you are to stop Murray by any means necessary, even if you have to hit him on the back of the head and sit on him."

"That's ganking-a-superior-officer, Sarge," said Blanchett.

"It's in a good cause, Blanchett, and that's an order. If the wizard gets me, you two go back home, pick up Sings-to-Trees here, and go find Algol."

"You can get court-martialed for ganking-a-superior-officer," said Blanchett.

"I'm telling you, Blanchett, it's on my orders."

Blanchett screwed up his face in the bear-listening position. "He says . . if you're dead, it won't matter if it was on your orders."

Nessilka pinched the bridge of her nose and prayed for patience, no less so because the bear was probably right.

". . . but he also says to do it," finished Blanchett. "So that's all right then, Sarge."

"As long as we're all in agreement," said Nessilka wearily, and shoved moss and wax into her ears.

THEY LEFT BLANCHETT un-earplugged, since he apparently wasn't affected, and he had flatly refused to wear them unless the bear got a pair, too. As the bear didn't really have much in the way of ear canals, it just seemed easier that way. There was enough crude hand-sign available in Glibber to be able to communicate simple orders, and Nessilka didn't feel like a complicated philosophical discussion at the moment anyway.

Sings-to-Trees halted under the last trees, gazing out

across the waving fields of the farmland. He frowned and said something, and then when Nessilka pulled out an earplug, he repeated himself. "The melons haven't been harvested. That strip along the drainage ditch—they always grow melons; it's got the most moisture—but they all split on the ground and rotted."

"How long does it take for melons to go bad?" asked Murray, who had also removed an earplug.

"About five minutes, sometimes," said Sings-to-Trees. "But these should have been harvested a few days ago, I think." He frowned.

Nessilka nodded. "Well, that gives us more of a time frame." She reached up and patted the elf on the shoulder. "Try to stay out of sight. Hopefully we'll be back before long."

They put in their earplugs, looked at each other awkwardly, then Nessilka nodded sharply and signed, *Move out.*

There was a main road not far away and a hedgerow running along one side of it. They stuck to it as closely as possible. It was taller than a goblin and made Nessilka feel less exposed. Small birds hopped through it. Murray pointed to one, and Nessilka nodded.

So it wasn't all the animals, then. That was something, anyway.

They crossed three fields and were midway through the fourth when they found the dead body.

Murray saw it first, in the drainage ditch. He stopped short, and Nessilka and Blanchett came up on either side of him and looked down and saw it, too.

It was a human child, very young. Nessilka couldn't do ages on humans at all, but it didn't look old enough to walk very well yet. It was lying in the bottom of the ditch with its eyes open and flies buzzing around it.

Nessilka's sigh sounded strange and muffled to herself with the moss in her ears. Blanchett looked as inscrutable as his teddy bear.

It was the enemy, but it was awfully small.

It fell in the ditch and couldn't get out again, she thought grimly. *Probably following the voice and not able to look where it was going.* She wondered where it had come from—she'd glimpsed a farmhouse far across the field on the other side of the road, through gaps in the hedgerow—but if it had come from there, had human adults come with it?

Of course, an adult could just step out of the drainage ditch . . .

Murray caught her eye and gestured to the farmhouse, then to the child. Nessilka turned her hands up and nodded, then shrugged. *Probably. I don't know.*

Nessilka gestured for them to move on. They couldn't take the time to bury the human, and anyway, humans usually burned their dead, didn't they? They certainly didn't have time for that, or the wood either, and a column of smoke would announce their approach as clearly as a bagpipe corps.

They moved on.

Two fields over, they found a dead dog. It looked old and not healthy. There was a trail of broken corn stalks behind it, and crows had been at its eyes.

Whatever it is, it doesn't affect crows, then.

Shading her eyes, Nessilka could see the town on the horizon. She wondered how many corpses there would be between here and there.

As it turned out, there were a lot. A horse with a broken leg had hauled itself an astonishingly long way and then fallen down, and by the torn-up ground, it had apparently tried to *crawl,* which Nessilka couldn't even imagine. A dead pig had expired without a mark on it, leaving a drainage ditch full of piglets that had probably died of starvation.

The sheep were really bad. Nessilka had seen a lot of horrible things in battle, but the entire flock of sheep had apparently run into a fence and gotten their heads stuck between slats, and then had beaten themselves to death against the fence posts. One or two were nearly decapitated.

Murray eyed them coolly, then turned to the sergeant and pulled an earplug loose. Nessilka followed suit, wincing.

"All domestic animals," he said. "Cats, too, which I suppose aren't really domesticated, but nothing really *wild*, anyway. Whatever this is, it's not affecting deer or rabbits or wild birds, just the farm animals."

"And people," said Nessilka grimly.

"And people."

They put their earplugs back in and kept moving, keeping low to the hedgerow. A flock of vultures had descended on a dead cow, which had smashed several fences and then been trampled by the rest of the herd.

There was another human, not far beyond it, who looked to also have been trampled by the cows.

After that, the humans became more frequent, the bodies more densely packed. Sometimes they appeared to have crawled over each other. Nessilka stopped seeing them. It was just like a battlefield the day after, a deep silence that seemed only to deepen behind the buzz of the flies and the croaking of the carrion birds.

They reached the farthest outlying building.

It was a little house, with a dead man lying on the front walk. He was very old, with white hair around his temples.

They were nearly abreast of him when the dead man moved.

It wasn't much, just a hand scrabbling at the packed dirt, but that was enough.

They stopped. It was one thing not to bury bodies; it was quite another to pass up a wounded man. They gathered around him. Nessilka pulled out an earplug, but held up a hand when Murray started to remove his.

"Help me," the old human rasped in a dialect that Nessilka could understand, even if the accent was strange. "Help me. Oh *please* . . ."

She crouched down next to him. "What happened here?" she asked.

His eyes were nearly closed and rimed with dried tears, but he cracked them open and squinted at her.

"Goblin?" he asked weakly. "You . . . you didn't do this to us . . ."

It didn't sound like a question. "No," said Nessilka. "We don't know what's happened, either." She pulled her water bottle off her belt and gave him a drink, trickling the water between his cracked lips. "Can you tell us anything?"

"Goblins," he said, sounding almost wondering. "Some kind of . . . weapon?"

"It wasn't us." She gave him a little more water and would have asked him more, but he sank into unconsciousness. She looked up at Murray helplessly.

"We'll come back for him if we can," said Murray, too loudly on account of the earplugs. "We should keep moving, Sarge."

Which was true. Which Murray shouldn't have had to tell her.

"Move him into the shade, at least." She and Murray each took a side and carried him back inside the house. There was a pallet on the floor—not much of one, but better than the walkway.

"Right. Let's move. Blanchett, if you hear anyone crying out, let us know." He nodded. She put her earplugs back in.

There were cattle in the town square. Some of the humans had died when the cattle crushed them. It was a mess, a horrible mess, which was a laughably ineffective word for the scene before them.

At least if she thought of it as *mess*, she didn't have to think of it as *people*.

Nessilka was glad Sings-to-Trees hadn't come. Or Algol. She didn't know if the elf could handle it, and while she knew Algol had been on battlefields, at least everybody there had been trying to kill you *back*.

There probably wasn't much point in sneaking, but they kept to the shadows and the corners of buildings anyway.

Murray tapped her shoulder, and she pulled the earplug

loose again—really, why was she bothering? The moss was coming unwrapped by now—and whispered, "Yes?"

"Eleven humans so far," he whispered back. "Maybe more in the buildings, but I don't think too many. They all seem to be trying to get into the town."

"Where are they going?"

Murray leaned out from the shadow of the building and pointed. "At a guess, that building there."

They studied the building in question.

"Pointy," said Blanchett finally.

"It's a steeple. Some kind of church, I think. In a town like this, probably the main meeting hall, too."

"All right. Stay low. We're in enemy territory, and don't anybody forget it," said Nessilka.

Murray looked around and said, "How could we forget, Sarge?"

They skulked from the shadow of one building to another. Nessilka thought that one was probably a bar, judging from the smell of spilled beer and rotting sawdust. She crouched behind a rain barrel and looked over at the church.

"The bear doesn't like it," said Blanchett suddenly.

Nessilka paused. "Does the bear have any suggestions?" she asked delicately.

Blanchett conferred with the bear and said, "He says not. Just . . . it feels like a trap. Not for us, maybe, but for *everybody*."

"I hate this," said Nessilka to no one in particular. "Tell the bear I agree with him. If he has any thoughts, tell me immediately."

"Will do, Sarge."

They crept closer.

The greatest concentration of the dead was at the end of the street, where the church sat in what had formerly been a village square. They were pressed right up against the walls of the church, close to the doors. They looked like they'd trampled each other, and then the cows had trampled *them*. In a couple of places there were three or four bodies piled together.

The church had big wooden double doors. The worst concentration of bodies was around the doors, and what looked like most of a steer had beaten itself to death against one, blockading it with a half ton of rotting meat.

The other door was ajar.

She and Murray exchanged glances. She had to fight the urge to meet the teddy bear's single button eye as well.

"Somebody moved those bodies away from the door," Murray hissed.

"Going in or coming out, that's the—ah!" She grabbed Murray's shoulder and yanked him back into the shadows.

A small figure—taller than a goblin, but not so broad—came out of a building across the square. It wore a cloth over its head and a bright blue coat. Its arms were full of . . . groceries? Nessilka could make out the corner of a sack of flour and some jars of preserves.

The goblins watched, hardly daring to breathe, as the figure looked around the square, then threaded its way nonchalantly through the bodies toward the open door.

"Human," whispered Murray. "Sub-adult. Can't do the genders from here."

"How can it even breathe?" asked Nessilka. The stench of the piled bodies was enough to knock her over, and she was twenty yards away and a goblin to boot.

"Maybe it's had time to get used to it."

The figure stopped at the door, balanced the load of groceries on one hip, and pushed the door open with its free hand.

One of the corpses shifted slightly when the door hit it, a limp arm flopping in the dust. The figure shoved the arm aside with its foot, caught the door with the edge of its shoulder, and slipped inside.

The goblins sat in the shadow of the building. Nessilka crouched behind a water barrel on the edge of the street and stared at the building.

Nothing happened.

"Maybe its parents are dead, and it's just trying to eat until someone gets here to find it," she said, without much conviction.

"Uh-huh," said Murray.

"The bear is pretty sure that's a load, Sarge," said Blanchett.

She sighed. "Yeah, me too." The casual way it had moved the corpse aside with its foot—that screamed "murderer" and "bad" and "do not touch."

"Think it's a wizard?"

"It'd almost have to be, wouldn't it?"

"There could be a grown-up wizard in there doing the actual magic." Murray chewed at his lower lip.

"Children are vicious little bastards, some of 'em," offered Blanchett.

Flies buzzed. Across the square, two crows got into a brief squabble over a tasty bit of carrion.

"Now what do we do, Sarge? Go back?" Murray glanced behind them.

Nessilka would have loved to go back. Going back sounded like a *great* idea.

But if they went back and told Sings-to-Trees, he'd insist on coming out to see if the human really was a child who needed help, and if his rangers showed up, they'd probably do the same, and if it was a goblin child, they'd be on their guard, but since it was a *human* and humans were *nice* . . .

There were already a whole lot of dead people out there. Nessilka didn't care very much for faceless unknown rangers, particularly not elves, but Sings-to-Trees didn't deserve to wind up in that pile of bodies.

And the Nineteenth—what there was of it—still had to get home, and if the weird voice magic could reach as far as the tree line, then they'd have to go *miles* out of their way to get home, and that would undoubtedly lead them into trouble with somebody who wasn't nearly as nice as Sings-to-Trees.

"We have to get a better look. Murray, you and me—Blanchett, stay here."

"Sarge..."

It was a poor day when Blanchett was questioning orders, Nessilka thought grimly. Still—"You're the only one we know is immune, so you're the only one who can get a message back if it gets us. If it's a kid... fine. If it's a grown-up wizard... well, we'll find out."

Blanchett hunched his shoulders and looked mulish, but perhaps the bear had a word with him, because he said gloomily "If you say so, Sarge."

She took one final look at the church and the bodies, shoved her earplugs back in—Murray did the same—and made a *move out* gesture with her fingers.

Nessilka and Murray moved out.

Sings-to-Trees stood just inside the forest and fretted.

He'd lost sight of the goblins fairly quickly—for all their apparent clumsiness, they knew their way around a hedgerow.

He hoped they would be okay.

He couldn't believe he'd nearly attacked the cervidian.

He should go back to the farm and send a pigeon. He should send a pigeon about the mage, and about the weird noise. The goblins would be fine. The goblins could take care of themselves.

Sings wrung his hands together.

The goblins could probably take care of themselves better than Sings himself could.

It was so *quiet*. The quiet bothered him almost as much as the memory of the voice did. Forest edges were hopping with life—birds and bugs and lizards and squirrels. There should be scurrying and scuttling and chirping and singing.

There should be—

Something stamped.

He turned his head slowly, already knowing what he would see.

Ah.

Yes.

The empty eyes of the cervidian stag stared back him.

"I won't go out there," he told the stag. "It's okay."

The stag rattled and stamped again.

"Er? Is there something else?"

He looked for the bone doe, but she wasn't there. Perhaps the stag had seen her somewhere safe, then returned.

The stag paced toward him. Sings held his ground. *I almost attacked him. He didn't attack me, and he didn't hurt that goblin, even though he could have. If anything, he's got the moral high ground on me.*

A few feet away, the cervidian halted. Hollow eyes gazed into his.

And then the stag turned slightly, stretched out a forelimb, and . . . knelt?

Why is he—

"Oh *no*," Sings-to-Trees said out loud. "Oh no! Ride you? You can't be serious!"

The stag rattled with impatience.

Sings-to-Trees eyed the exposed knobs of the stag's backbone and imagined then against his tender bits. He shuddered.

"Are you sure I can't just follow you?"

The stag rattled again and pawed at the ground.

"I'll—but your back—oh, dear . . ."

Sings-to-Trees was not any more fond of pain than any elf, but he had chosen a life that involved a certain degree of personal discomfort. It appeared that this was going to involve more of the same.

He looked at the stag's backbone again.

Very . . . *personal* . . . discomfort.

He saved us before. I healed his mate. He clearly knows more about the magic that's going on than I do.

Oh, dear . . .

"Half a moment," said Sings-to-Trees. He stripped off his tunic and began packing grass and moss into it. There was no putting a saddle on a cervidian, but perhaps he could manage some slight protection between himself and the jut of the stag's vertebrae.

The cervidian waited. Sings-to-Trees finished stuffing his makeshift pillow, took a deep breath, and prepared to ride the bone stag into the unknown.

THE VILLAGE SQUARE felt agonizingly exposed. The goblins clung to the shadow of the buildings as long as they could, and then there was a water trough for horses partway there, but after that there was nothing to hide behind except bodies.

It was not the first time in Nessilka's life she'd hidden behind bodies, but if the great gibbering gods were kind, it'd be the last. She thought the smell might follow her for *several* lifetimes.

She and Murray crouched behind a cow. It was bloated and its tongue was sticking out. Its udder had puffed up like a balloon. She had never given much thought to what happened to a cow's udder when it rotted. She wished she wasn't giving it any thought now.

Murray jerked his chin at the door. It was still slightly ajar, and there was no cover between them and it, unless you counted the dead steer blocking the other door. They could hide behind the open door, but there were bodies there, and they'd have to actually climb on them and . . . no.

The dead steer it would have to be.

She flicked her fingers. *Going. Cover me.*

That last dash across the open square made her nerves jangle like badly tuned bells. Goblin feet were large and flat and actually fairly good for stealth if you moved carefully and didn't let them go slap-slap-slap, but there were patches of . . . mud. *Let's go with mud. Red mud. Yes.* She had to be careful not to squelch. And how was Murray going to cover her, anyway? Throw a dead body at anyone who attacked her?

She fetched up behind the dead steer and waited with her heart in her throat.

Nothing happened.

Flies buzzed around her in a cloud, but no strange voice called out. Nobody came to see what was going on or to scream because there was a goblin warrior in town.

Oh, this would be a bad time for the rangers to show up . . . Thirty-odd dead bodies and three live goblins . . . no, that didn't bear thinking about.

Murray crossed the square and dropped down beside her.

They exchanged glances, then looked at the gap in the door. It was about six inches wide and yawned like a chasm before them.

She flicked a finger at Murray—*wait*—and sidled to the edge of the door.

It was dark inside. The bright sunlight made hot bars of light across the shadows, illuminating the edge of a pew. She crouched low, squinting.

It was hard to see anything. *Well, no help for it . . .* She took out an earplug.

There was a faint sizzling sound in the darkness. It was a familiar enough sound, but so far out of normal context that she couldn't place it.

The smell of the dead was overwhelming, but under it, Nessilka could smell . . . pancakes?

She could make out a shape at the far end of the gloom, backlit by the remains of a fire, and in front of the embers, humming—*humming?*—was the human subadult, and *it was frying pancakes.*

Goblins were occasionally bad. Goblins were scourges of the night. And war was war, and after a battle you generally ate like a starving wolf although you couldn't always keep it down afterward.

But even goblins didn't stand in buildings surrounded by the piled dead and make pancakes.

She felt a brief, blinding rage—humans might be the

enemy, but these were *civilians*, goddamnit—and then the rage died away and was replaced with a deep, unsettled disquiet.

Because anybody who would do that was crazy—bad, bugshit crazy, deep-down crazy. Not like wizards, who were mostly just normal people whose heads didn't always work right, but somebody who's soul was back to front and possibly sideways. People like that had a rabid animal in their head, and you could see it gnawing at the back of their eyes when they talked.

And they were very, very dangerous because there was absolutely no telling what they would do next.

She didn't look back at Murray. Her eyes would have to adjust again if she did. And she couldn't sign what she was seeing—goblin hand-sign did not include things like "psychopath making pancakes."

She gritted her teeth and slipped inside.

The door did not quite creak when she pushed it open, but it let in more light, and if the human looked up, it was bound to see the difference. Nessilka dropped low behind the first pew, breathing silently through her mouth, listening.

There was no change in the humming. It was a tuneless little repetition, hmm-hmm-hmm-hm-hm-hmm-hm, in no particular order.

Why don't I have a crossbow? I could shoot it from here and save us all the trouble. She should have borrowed one from Sings-to-Trees. Surely he had one for dealing with . . . something. Rabid foxes or rogue deer or whatever.

She crept the length of the pew, shot another look at the fire—it appeared to be made out of broken chairs and cushions from the pews—and looked for the human. It had moved a foot or two to one side and was fumbling with something on the ground.

Probably wants syrup on its pancakes, she thought darkly.

She took the chance and scurried to the next pew, and then she heard a quiet *glug* and had a hysterical urge to laugh, because that was exactly the sound of somebody pouring out syrup.

The tuneless humming stopped and was replaced by the scrape of fork on plate and the sounds of chewing. Nessilka doubted she would have been able to hear either if the town had not been so deadly silent.

Did she dare risk another pew?

She had just decided to go down the length of the pew to the far end and use that concealment to move forward when she heard the door creak.

It was louder this time, and damn it, Murray still had his earplugs in, so *of course* he didn't hear it, and if they got out of this alive, she was going to box his ears—

The eating noises stopped.

"Hello?" said a voice, shockingly close. Cloth rustled as the human stood up. "Is someone there?"

She stood up. If the human fixed on her, maybe it would overlook Murray.

It was standing less than five feet away. It still had a fork and a plate of pancakes in its hand. Blond hair poked out from under the cloth on its head, and it—she?—stared at Sergeant Nessilka with wide blue eyes.

"Um," Nessilka said. "Hi?"

"You're a *goblin*," said the human girl, sounding strangely aggrieved, as if she had been expecting someone else.

"Goblin," said Nessilka. "Yes. Absolutely. Born and bred. You can tell by the feet, see?"

She held up a foot. This was not strictly necessary, as any idiot could have identified Nessilka as a goblin at a hundred paces, but while the girl was looking at her foot, she was not looking at Murray, who had damn well better be hunkering down behind a pew and pretending to be a prayer book.

"It wasn't supposed to be *goblins*," said the girl.

"Um. Sorry." Nessilka was not going to go for her club. It would probably be sensible to go for her club, and she knew this human was going to be bad news—innocent bystanders did not make pancakes while surrounded by the piled dead—but it was surprisingly hard to hit a kid who wasn't doing anything but staring at you. Even a human kid.

I am going to regret this later, thought Nessilka, *I know I am, but I'm still not going for my club, what am I, stupid, why am I not going for my club . . . ?*

"So . . . are you here all alone?" she asked instead.

"Oh, *yes*," said the girl, a faint tremor in her voice. "The wizard came and—it was horrible—all those people—" She put her face in her hands, and her hair fell down over it in a perfect picture of misery.

Nessilka did not buy this for a second. She supposed it was possible that it was just because humans were The Enemy, but all her sergeanting instincts told her there was a little too much practice in that delivery. If a new recruit had come to her with that kind of theatrics, she'd have knocked him down and had Thumper sit on him until he told the truth.

"I'm an *orphan*," sobbed the girl.

"So am I," said Nessilka. "We could bond, if you like."

Somehow she didn't think the girl was going to take her up on the offer.

"The wizard said these words..."

"Wizard, hmm?" She folded her arms and leaned against the back of the pew. She was pretty sure the girl was watching her from behind her hands and that curtain of hair. "Where did he go?"

"It was so awful! He said these words, and—all those *people*—"

"Yes, yes," said Nessilka, "you said that bit already." She caught a glimpse of Murray peeking out behind the pew and gave him a death glare. He had the grace to look ashamed, mouthed *Sorry, Sarge*, and pulled back out of sight.

"He left," said the girl, sniffling. "And then everybody was dead, and my brother is gone, and I was all alone—"

"Overlooked you, hmm?" Nessilka began wandering down the aisle toward the altar. Anything to get her eyes away from Murray—maybe he'd be able to slip out the door, not that she could trust him to do anything so sensible...

"I th-think so..." The girl took her hands away from her face. "Please, you must save me! Take me away from here, before he returns!"

"Door's open," said Nessilka. "Why didn't you just leave and go for help?"

"L-leave?" This clearly took her by surprise. *Didn't rehearse that part of your speech, did you?*

"Seems a bit weird to stay here and make breakfast while you wait for this wizard of yours to come back."

The girl's eyes narrowed. "You're not very nice," she said. "It's been horrible, and I'm the *sold survivor*—"

"*Sole* survivor," said Murray, who had never in his life been able to resist correcting someone's grammar.

Nessilka winced and wondered when he'd taken out the useless earplugs.

Murray coughed apologetically and stood up. "And you're actually not," he said. "There's at least one old guy in a little house on the edge of town who could probably pull through with a bit of water and some tending."

"What?" This information somehow did not seem to gratify the human at all. "Old Man Houghton? How—" Her face smoothed out, and she said, in a much different tone, "Oh. That's wonderful, of course!"

Nessilka and Murray glanced at each other.

"You don't know! It's been horrible!" said the girl, and burst into furious tears.

Were all human civilians this *wet*? Nessilka didn't much like humans to begin with, what with the taking-her-homeland bit and lately the always-trying-to-kill-her bit, but she'd give the human soldiers this—they didn't cry at you. Not until you'd cut their legs off, anyway, and that didn't count.

"Uh, Sarge . . ." said Murray.

The human sobbed.

"There there, yes, you've suffered terribly. 'Scuse us a minute," said Nessilka, grabbing Murray by the arm. She yanked him back toward the door and hissed, in furious Glibber, "*Are you out of your mind?*"

"I think she's the one who did it, Sarge!"

"Well, *obviously*! And I ought to bust you back down to private for disobeying orders!"

"But Sarge, I think—"

"You're not going to work," said the girl, in a clear, carrying voice without a trace of a sob.

Nessilka wheeled around and found that the girl was

between them and the door. Her hand dropped instinctively to the haft of her club.

"You're not supposed to be here," said the girl. "You were *supposed* to be elves. The elves were supposed to come and take me away to find John, and you're just going to ruin *everything*."

The human's eyes were very bright. *Crazylight*, thought Nessilka. *Sane people's eyes don't look like that unless they're dying.*

"Let's not do anything rash," said Murray, spreading his hands. "We can talk about this—"

Ten steps, thought Nessilka. *Over the back of the pew and ten steps and then club her.*

"You won't work at all," said the girl. "And if Old Man Houghton's still kicking around—what a *mess*." She sounded annoyed, but her crazylight eyes gleamed, and Nessilka knew that she was probably already too late.

The sergeant lunged.

She got over the back of the pew and two steps farther, and that was all. The girl opened her mouth and tilted her head back a little, and a sound came out.

It was that maddening, half-heard conversation sound, but louder and closer and painful. The words cut right through the center of Nessilka's head like the teeth of a bone saw. The human's lips were hardly moving but her throat was vibrating strangely and great gibbering gods Nessilka wanted to go toward it, it was *important* that she go toward it, but it hurt, it felt like the two halves of her skull were grating together and the girl was backing away from them but she had to get closer, perhaps if she could just hear what the voice was saying the horrible grating in her head would stop because if it didn't stop the bones in Nessilka's ears were going to shatter and she was going to go deaf and why was she moving so slowly, because the girl was backing out the door but her feet seemed to stick to the floor and Murray was moaning and she wanted to smack him because his moaning was making it harder to make out the words and oh gods, why hadn't she used the club when she had a chance—

And then Blanchett brought his club down on the back of the girl's head.

The sound cut off instantly. There was a thump as the human wizard—she couldn't have been anything else—folded up and hit the ground. Nessilka heard herself cry out in anguish and relief. So did Murray.

She staggered to the door and looked out. The one-eyed teddy bear bobbed atop the helmet. "Sorry, Sarge," said Blanchett, "but he said you needed some help."

"Tell him he's promoted," rasped Nessilka. "I'll get him some stripes."

"He'd like that, Sarge."

Murray looked down at the crumpled human and nudged her with one flat foot. The human groaned. "You didn't kill her," he said.

"Was I supposed to?"

"Might have made things easier. What are we going to do now, Sarge?"

Nessilka looked at the unconscious wizard, looked at the pile of bodies, looked up at Murray—and was spared any kind of decision because at that moment, the rangers arrived.

There is a game that most civilized creatures play in times of great turmoil, which might best be called "How Boned Are We?"

Nessilka and Murray were playing it now.

"We're boned," said Murray.

"Yup," said Nessilka.

"They're gonna think we did all of it."

"Sings-to-Trees will set them straight."

"If they think to ask him."

"True."

"And there's no chance they'll believe the kid did it."

"Doesn't look like it, no."

"So we're boned."

"Yup."

Blanchett was sitting this one out, since the elves had taken their weapons, and his fanged orc-helmet seemed to qualify. Without the bear, Blanchett was as silent as the grave.

Nessilka had made an effort. When she'd been kneeling in the mud with a sword held near her neck and an elf had been trussing her up with grim efficiency, she'd said, "That bear is one of my men. I demand that you treat him with the courtesy due to a prisoner of war."

Which had gone over about as well as you'd expect, but at least she'd seen bear, helmet, and weapons vanish into a sack together. So that was something. Leave no soldier behind and all.

They hadn't been killed on the spot, and that was also something.

She was pretty sure that goblins were considered generally too incompetent to pull off something like this.

Pretty sure.

Fairly sure, anyway.

Reasonably hopeful.

She'd told them the kid was a wizard. She wasn't sure if they'd listened. Probably not. They'd whisked the girl away somewhere, and realistically, the three enemies of the state standing in the town full of bodies, having just clubbed one of the last survivors, were not the most credible of witnesses.

They had been removed from the village and dropped in a sheep pasture about a half mile distant. Somebody had set up a tent, and she could smell a fire burning on the other side of the hedgerow. A silent elf with a crossbow was standing guard.

"Do you speak this language?" he had asked. (He had asked probably the same question three other times, in what sounded like three other languages, but Nessilka didn't know any of them. She was interested to note that it was not the language the human had spoken, so perhaps the races didn't have that much contact after all.)

"Yes," she said. Murray nodded. Blanchett stared into the distance.

"Good. I am very angry. If you attempt to escape, I will be very glad to kill you. Do you understand me?"

They nodded.

"We didn't do it," said Murray hopelessly.

"You will have a chance to speak to Captain Finchbones in your defense," said the elf, and then walked five feet away and became as communicative as a stone.

"We're boned," said Murray glumly.

"Yup."

"Think we can escape?"

"No."

"If the kid does the thing—"

"Then we'll break our necks trying to get to her, most likely, if we don't get trampled by the elves first. Unless it doesn't work on elves." She looked at their captor. His hair was perfect. You could braid enough coup markers in that hair to account for a small berserker nation.

They sat in the sheep pasture and watched the sun crawl across the sky.

Nessilka tried to engage Blanchett. "Blanchett? Can you hear the bear?"

No response.

Great grim gods, what if his brain is melted? What if this is what drives him over the edge?

More over the edge?

"Blanchett, I want you to listen to me. The bear is on a very important mission. He's doing reconnaissance. You need to stay with me until the bear reports back, understand?"

He turned his head half an inch toward her. Nessilka felt a sudden enormous relief, capture by the enemy notwithstanding. She wriggled into a more comfortable position and leaned toward Blanchett.

The elf's crossbow went *click*.

She leaned back and addressed the sky. "Blanchett, I know you're in there. You just need to sit tight until the bear comes back, okay?"

His lips moved. It might have been *Yes, Sarge*. It might have been almost anything.

The tent flap was pulled back, and two more elves emerged. Nessilka sized them up as they approached. Was one Captain Finchbones?

"The one in the armor?" guessed Murray.

"No," said Nessilka, who knew a bit more about command. "The one who looks tired."

And indeed, of the two elves approaching, one looked exhausted. His shoulders were stooped, and his long white hair made him look old instead of ethereal.

He had weary eyes. Nessilka clenched her fingers together.

If you are going to be captured—and if you are a goblin soldier, this is always at least a possibility—it is rarely a good idea to be captured by tired people. Tired people make mistakes. Those mistakes are rarely in your favor. For every guard who dozes off or who fails to lock the prison door, you get a dozen guards who forget that they've taken the safety off the crossbow, who mistake a plea for water for an assault, or who fail to loosen the ropes before somebody's hand turns black and falls off.

Tired commanders are even worse. Tired commanders have a tendency to want problems to just go away.

Nessilka knew that she, Murray, Blanchett, and a town full of corpses added up to a very *big* problem.

The tired elf squatted down in the mud in front of her—he was wearing very good boots—and said, "I am Captain Finchbones."

"Point to you, Sarge," muttered Murray.

"Do you understand this language?"

"Yes," said Nessilka. She licked dry lips and wracked her brain, trying to remember vocabulary. "Most. Need you explain some words."

Finchbones nodded. "I wish to make sure there are no misunderstandings. Explain to me why you were in the village."

Nessilka hardly knew where to begin. "We were in woods. We heard very strange noise." Should she mention Sings-to-Trees? If they went to his farm, they'd find the rest of the regiment. Damn. "A magic noise. We had to walk to it."

"Why were you in the woods?" asked Finchbones.

"A wizard"—damn, what was the word for *transported?*—"moved us."

Finchbones eyebrows went up at that. "A goblin wizard?"

"No!" That was all they needed, to have the elves thinking that they had wizards that could dump whole regiments behind enemy lines. "No. Human."

"Why did a human wizard send you into my people's lands?"

Murray muttered, "Careful, Sarge . . ." in Glibber. The elf behind him made a warning noise.

Nessilka sighed. There was really no answer that was going to paint them in a positive light. It was best to be honest. At least if they were prisoners of war, there were supposed to be rules about how they were treated.

"In battle. Ran at wizard." Her hands were tied, but she managed a vague pantomime of attack with her head and one shoulder. Finchbones nodded. "Wizard moved. We moved too. Then we were in woods."

Murray cleared his throat. Apparently he spoke this human dialect better than he spoke Elvish. "We think he was trying to run from the battle, but he brought all of us with him."

Nessilka winced a little at *all of us*, but presumably that could apply to three people as easily as nine.

Finchbones shifted so that he was addressing both Murray and Nessilka. "Where is this wizard now?"

Nessilka shook her head. "Asleep." That wasn't the right word, but it was as close as she was going to get. "Left wizard asleep in woods."

"Dead?"

"No!"

"Unconscious," said Murray.

Finchbones nodded.

Nessilka tried to explain that they'd given the wizard some water and put a blanket over him, but she wasn't sure how much of that came through, or whether Finchbones believed her.

She hated not being able to speak clearly. It made her sound stupid, and people thought goblins were stupid enough already.

"Who is in command?"

"I am," said Nessilka. "I am—" She looked helplessly at Murray.

"Sergeant," said Murray.

"Sergeant Nessilka. I am in command." She licked her lips again. "I ask . . . fair. Fairness. Treatment of soldiers."

"Prisoners of war," said Finchbones.

Nessilka nodded. So did Murray.

Finchbones steepled his fingers. "And yet the people you have killed were not soldiers."

"Did not kill people!"

Murray said, "The village was like that already. Already dead."

"Days," said Nessilka. "Many days dead. And we only three goblins." She jerked her chin at Blanchett and Murray.

"You were found standing over a girl with a club," said Finchbones grimly. "Making pancakes."

Part of Nessilka was enormously gratified that the elf could see how wrong it was to make pancakes while surrounded by dead bodies. This was largely mitigated by the fact that he thought they were *her* pancakes.

"Not us. Girl."

"She is a wizard," said Murray. "She made the noise."

Nessilka stared up into Finchbones's eyes, willing him to believe her. Because if he didn't . . . Well, it was going to be unpleasant for the goblins in the short term, and for everybody in the long term.

Finchbones made a noncommittal noise and stood up. "I am not sure that I believe you."

Nessilka sighed. "Wouldn't believe either," she said. "Hear magic noise, *then* believe."

"By then it'll be too late," said Murray.

Finchbones lifted his other eyebrow. "You will be brought water," he said. "Do not try to escape."

Nessilka snorted. "Where we go?"

"There's that," said Finchbones, and walked away.

Sings-to-Trees had found the wizard, for all the good it was doing him.

He hadn't been hard to find. The cervidian had dumped Sings directly in front of the young human's campfire. It wasn't a large campfire, but it was perfectly serviceable, and the wizard was feeding it twigs and making no attempt to hide the smoke or his presence in the forest.

Sings could tell it was the wizard because he was still wearing Nessilka's cloak. Badly cured goat hide clashed oddly with the human's military uniform.

Also, the wizard's response to having a skeletal deer leap in front of him and a bruised and whimpering elf fall off its back was to say, "Oh."

That was it. He didn't even make eye contact with Sings-to-Trees. (This was all very well, as far as Sings was concerned, because he didn't really want someone looking at him right at that moment. He was curled around bruises that would have felled a trained warrior, let alone a veterinarian.)

The cervidian rattled and stamped a hoof. The wizard fed another twig to the fire.

Sings sat up and said, "Are you the wizard?"

The wizard looked at his face briefly, and then back at the fire. "Yes?" He sounded unsure about it.

"Did you come through a"—Sings had to stop and translate mentally from the goblin tongue—"a hole in the air?"

"Yes?"

"There were goblins with you."

The wizard nodded. "Lots of them," he said. "I ran away. They came with me through the hole." He gave Sings-to-Trees a brief, determined look. "I make holes."

"Good for you," said Sings. "Are you injured?"

"No?"

"The goblins said you were unconscious."

The wizard nodded again. "Lots of them came through the hole. They were very heavy."

Sings realized this was all the explanation he was going

to get. "My name is Sings-to-Trees."

"My name is John."

"I live here, in the woods. A few miles away."

John was silent for so long that Sings-to-Trees started thinking of another question, but then the wizard seemed to realize that something else was expected of him. "I live in the village. Elliot's Cross?"

He looked worried. Sings said, "That's a nice place," and the wizard visibly relaxed.

Poor soul. He's trying. People like this shouldn't be in wars, even if they are good at it.

"Were you trying to get back there?"

"Yes? But lots of them came through the hole." He furrowed his brow. Sings had an impression not so much of lack of intelligence, but of lack of ability to communicate. Sings wondered whether it was the language barrier, or if there simply weren't words for the magical concepts in his head. "When . . . when too many go through the hole . . . the hole won't go far."

"I understand, I think," said Sings. *Elliot's Cross is what the humans call their village, isn't it? He was trying to escape the battle and go back home, but when the goblins fell through, he only got partway there, and it took so much energy it knocked him out. Makes sense, I guess, as much as anything with magic makes sense.*

"There's some very strange magic happening in the woods here," said Sings. "It attracted the cervidian." He nodded to the stag. It rattled.

"Okay?" Again that inquiring lift at the end of the word. John darted a look at the elf's face again.

Is he asking questions? He doesn't seem hostile; he just seems confused . . . Then again, if he took some kind of magical backlash, confusion might be the least of it.

"It isn't me," said the wizard. Not a question this time.

"It's bad magic," said Sings.

"It is?" He met the elf's eyes with an expression of naked entreaty. It reminded Sings, for a moment, of a troll, all good nature and confusion.

Then Sings had it, and his heart broke a little for the human, because he realized what the man was asking.

He knows he's supposed to react somehow when I tell him these things, and he doesn't know the right thing to say. Poor baffled soul. Worst case of magic I've seen in a while, and if Nessilka's right, and he's able to kill people with that blue stuff as well as "make holes," then probably most of what he learned was in the human army, and the gods only know what they poured into his head.

"It's killing people." said Sings. "It's bad. We don't like it."

The wizard nodded once, firmly, as if committing this to memory. "Sorry, sir," he said after a moment, sounding a bit less abstract. "I get confused sometimes. My magic . . . does things."

"That's okay," said Sings. "If I tell you about the magic here, can you tell me if you know anything about it?"

"Yes, sir." He lowered his head slightly and pulled the goblin cloak tight around his shoulders. Sings-to-Trees had the feeling that no one had ever listened to him so intently in his entire life. The forest itself seemed to quiet down, out of respect for the intensity of the wizard's concentration.

"It's some kind of sound. It's as if you can almost hear a conversation, but you can't make out the words. It makes you try to get closer, no matter who's in the way. People run toward it from miles away. In fact—"

He stopped there because John had sat bolt upright. More of the vagueness vanished from his face, replaced with dawning horror.

"It's Lisabet," he said, and it was clear he knew exactly how he felt about that. "That's her power. She makes the voice."

"Lisabet?" Now Sings-to-Trees was the one who didn't know how to feel about something. "Who's that?"

"My sister," said John. "We have to find her, sir." He didn't look vague at all now, just very worried and very determined. "It's very important that we find her at once. Before something terrible happens."

Their bonds had been loosened, and they had been given water. When the goblins were retied, the elves let them keep their hands in front. Nessilka debated requesting the teddy bear again, then decided not to push her luck.

"Do you think he believes us?" asked Murray.

"No."

"He has to know we couldn't have killed all those people. And they've been dead for days."

"He doesn't have any way to know how long we've been here." Nessilka sighed. "Think it through, Murray..."

He did. She saw his face fall. He scowled. Nessilka nodded.

"He's caught *us*. There could be dozens of goblins in the woods, and he just doesn't know it yet. We could have been transported here weeks ago. We could have been killing people all that time. We could have our own wizard with us." She considered this. "I'd be surprised if they hadn't heard that voice thing as they were approaching. That girl had a heckuva range."

Murray considered this. "I think she might have been focusing it on us. When we were hearing it before, it didn't give me that horrible headache, and we could move a lot faster."

Knowing that your enemy has the ability to focus her powers was somehow not comforting. Nessilka rested her forehead on her knees. "Well, regardless. They don't know how many of us there are. They may think we've got a wizard. Hell, maybe Blanchett here's a wizard, they don't know."

Blanchett focused his eyes with apparent difficulty and said, "No."

Nessilka forced a smile. "Glad to have you with us again, Blanchett."

"The bear?" he said.

"Still on a mission."

"I'll wait, then." He lay down on his side and, to all appearances, went to sleep.

Nessilka envied him.

A few minutes slid by, and then Murray said, "Sarge?"

"Mm?"

"It's worse than that. It may not matter if he believes us or not."

Nessilka glanced over at the tent. Late afternoon shadows stretched over the grass, but there was no movement. "It doesn't?"

The other goblin gestured as well as he could with his wrists bound together. "Look, there are people who don't like the war, right?"

"I'm not terribly fond of it myself, Murray."

"No, no. I mean *civilians*."

"Oh, them."

"Well . . . Sings-to-Trees thinks the war is bad. And there's probably more like him out there. Maybe not so many elves, but what about the humans? They're doing most of the fighting, and they're probably getting tired of it."

"The great grim gods know that I am." Nessilka glanced at their guard. He had not moved an inch in the last two hours. She had to watch for a minute to make sure he was blinking.

"So . . ." said Murray. "Say you've got people getting tired of the war. Then you get a bunch of goblins showing up and wiping out a whole human village. Do you think those people are still going to be tired of it?"

Nessilka scowled. "That's *politics*, Murray."

"Well, yeah. Lotta people die of politics."

She was suddenly very glad that she hadn't told the elf

captain about the rest of the regiment or about Sings-to-Trees.

They sat in the sheep pasture while the shadows grew so long that they joined up to each other and became evening.

"Hey, Murray?"

"Yes, Sarge?"

"Maybe they'll figure out we were right, and they'll give us medals."

"Very funny, Sarge."

Torches were lit outside the tent, and someone started a campfire. When Nessilka looked back to their guard, she saw his pupils dilated as wide as a cat's in the dark. It was an unsettling look. Goblin eyes didn't do that.

She engaged in a few moments of recreational xenophobia, which didn't help at all but did pass the time.

Someone came toward them with a torch. Nessilka was hoping for food, but it was Captain Finchbones again.

He did not crouch down this time, but said without preamble, "The human girl says that you and a wizard killed everyone in the village."

Nessilka shook her head. "No," she said.

Finchbones narrowed his eyes. "Where is this wizard?"

"Not us. Girl is wizard."

What's the point? They're not going to believe a couple of goblins. If Murray's right, it doesn't even matter if they do or not.

"Ask the old man," said Murray suddenly.

It took Nessilka a minute to remember what he was talking about—it had been that long a day—and then she sat up. "Yes! Old man! Old man alive, in house. Old man saw us. Gave him water."

And he may decide we're responsible. Or he may be dead. But I suppose it's better than nothing. At least he can testify we didn't kill him when we had the chance.

Murray nodded. "We told the wizard girl he was alive. She didn't like that."

Finchbones shook his head slowly. "It's very likely you are lying," he said, "but for the life of me, I can't figure out why you'd lie about this. It's easily checked, anyway."

He turned to the elf with the torch and issued a few short commands in Elvish. The man nodded and hurried away.

This left them in relative darkness. The elven captain's eyes dilated in the same fashion as the guard's. Nessilka hadn't noticed that effect with Sings-to-Trees, but she supposed she hadn't been paying attention.

What was Sings thinking, now that they hadn't shown up? Would Algol wait until Thumper had healed, then take the group of them to Goblinhome? They'd practically walk by the elven camp if they did . . .

"I will get to the bottom of this," said Finchbones. "I don't believe you were alone out here, and I think goblins turning up in a dead village is too much of a coincidence. But there are a great many things that don't add up, either."

Like how three goblins caused herds of farm animals to trample themselves to death, say?

No, I suppose they'll blame that on the hypothetical wizard we're apparently working for. Sigh.

"We are rangers," said Finchbones. "We can track a squirrel through a thousand-mile forest. We will find out where you came from and what has happened here."

Nessilka met his eyes squarely. "Good. Then will understand. Then will grant fairness as prisoners of war."

If you can grandstand, son, so can I . . . She only wished she had the words to do it well.

His eyes did not look tired any longer. He nodded once, turned on his heel, and left.

"Think he'll ask her about it?" asked Murray.

"If he does," said Nessilka, "I imagine we'll know in a few minutes."

NESSILKA'S ESTIMATE WAS off by almost an hour. Possibly Finchbones had been subtle with his questioning, or maybe he'd sent someone to go find the old human. Nessilka rather hoped that the old man had pulled through.

Somebody ought to, and our odds don't look good.

And then, just as the moon came up and sat on top of the hedgerow, the voice began again.

Oh hell . . . thought Nessilka.

Their guard's head jerked up, and without a glance at them, he began to walk toward the command tent.

This is our chance! We can escape! We can get away! We . . . Yeah, no, I'm crawling toward the tent, aren't I? Lovely.

The really obnoxious thing about this magic was how knowing what was happening to her didn't change anything. She knew perfectly well that there wasn't a conversation (oh but it was so close) that she'd never understand it (unless she got just a little bit closer, close enough to make out the words) that even if she did understand it (just a little closer) that it was coming from the throat of a deranged killer who'd destroyed an entire village, apparently as bait for a group of elves.

I wonder if they heard what she was actually saying before they died.

She tried to stand up, but the elves had hobbled her feet with such a short length of rope that crawling covered the ground more quickly. Murray shuffled along next to her.

"Sarge?" asked Blanchett, slow and puzzled, and Nessilka sank her teeth into her lower lip because she knew how hard it was for him to talk without the bear thinking for him but he was making it harder to hear the words and she could swear she almost got a full sentence that time, just about—

She put her arm in a gopher hole and went into it up to the shoulder. Murray crawled past her as she struggled to extricate herself. Then Blanchett went past with a very odd look on his face, except that he was going the wrong way— not toward the command tent at all, but veering off toward one of the other tents.

Nessilka managed to think: *He'll never get near the voice that way! Where is he going—oh, good thinking, Blanchett, good job*—and then she found herself shushing her own thoughts, trying to listen to the voice that was almost there, just a little closer, just up to the back of the command tent now...

There were elves pushing up against the walls of the tent. One lifted his sword to cut through the fabric, and then the voice changed—Nessilka stifled a scream—and now it was the same as it had been in the church, now it was painful, now the conversation was a buzz that was going to pry the tiny bones of her ears loose and throw them like jacks inside the chamber of her skull...

Murray, a few yards ahead, sank down to his belly and tried to shield his ears as best he could with his arms tied together at the wrist.

I wonder if this is how those people died...

A mountain of flesh passed in front of her vision.

Something picked her up, one-handed, and tucked her against what felt like a wall of warty skin. Nessilka's head was hurting terribly badly, and if she could just hear what the voice was saying, the pain would stop, that must be what it was talking about, how to stop the headache, but still—*what? Is something carrying me? How?*

The creature reached down and grabbed Murray, too, and then began moving toward the tent. Nessilka approved of this because it was getting her closer to the voice, and it was moving much faster than she could.

Her captor came around the side of the tent, and Nessilka saw the girl.

She was standing a few feet from the front of the tent, and there was a ring of elves around her, all of them on their knees or curled on their sides, holding their heads. Finchbones had a crossbow and was struggling to raise it, but his hands were shaking so badly that he couldn't even get it off the ground.

There was another creature there as well, like the one carrying Nessilka. It was holding a struggling Sings-to-Trees around the waist, and in its other arm—

She wasn't going to forget that human's face in a hurry. For one thing, he was still wearing her cloak.

The girl saw the wizard and snapped her mouth closed. "John!" she cried, dashing toward him.

Nessilka's brain felt like a crumpled ball of paper suddenly smoothed flat. The elves gave a collective moan of relief. Finchbones lifted the crossbow and fumbled with the bolt.

The large creature set the wizard down hurriedly. Sings-to-Trees, hanging limply in the monster's other arm, babbled something to it in Elvish.

The girl threw her arms around the wizard—John's—neck and said, somewhat muffled, "I knew it would work. I knew they'd have to bring you back if there was nobody else to take care of me."

Nessilka twisted her head and looked up at the creature holding her. Had it been immune to the noise?

It looked back down at her. It had a wide, froggy mouth and enormous eyes. It looked like a toad crossed with a bull crossed with a small hillside.

"Grah," it said cheerfully.

"They're trolls, Sarge," said Murray. "Sings-to-Trees talked about them. I think they're friends of his."

"Grah!"

"Where's Blanchett?" whispered Nessilka. "I don't want an elf shooting him if he's wandering off!"

"Haven't seen him, Sarge. Maybe he's on the other side of the tent?"

Finchbones managed to get the crossbow loaded and raised it up. "Sir," he said with a heavy accent, "must move back from her. Now."

Nessilka felt a distinct stab of pleasure that the elven captain spoke this dialect rather worse than she did. *Now who sounds unintelligent? Ha!*

Wizard and girl both ignored him. The wizard said, "Lisabet . . . what have you done?"

"Nothing!" said the girl. "Well, I shouldn't have had to do

anything! They shouldn't have taken you away!"

Finchbones tried again. "Sir. Move back. Now."

John not only didn't move back, he held Lisabet more tightly. Any crossbow bolt would go through both of them, and Nessilka was pretty sure the wizard knew it. "I'm sorry, sir," he said. "Did she do something bad?"

Finchbones looked tired and grim. "Killed. Killed... village, entire. Many killed. Move back."

"Lisabet!" The young wizard looked down at her.

"They wouldn't bring you back! I told them I'd do it if they didn't bring you back, and they didn't listen!"

Sings-to-Trees put his hands over his face, looking gray.

"I had to go away, Lisabet! It's—It's so much better. They explain things, and nobody's scared of me. You shouldn't have done this."

Finchbones said something to one of the other elves. The elf said, "The captain is warning you. You must step away from the girl. She is extremely dangerous, and we cannot guarantee your safety."

Lisabet glared up at her brother. "So you're *glad* you went away?"

The boy was a poor liar, Nessilka thought. She was another species, and even she could see the answer on his face.

"Fine!" yelled the girl. "Fine, if that's how it is! I'm sorry I ever wanted you to come back!"

The girl pulled back. Finchbones jerked the crossbow up.

She opened her mouth and made the noise again.

Nessilka had to give it to Captain Finchbones. His hands were shaking badly, and the shot went wild, but it went past her left shoulder with only inches to spare. And he did all this while everyone else was slamming their hands over their ears. The only reason that Nessilka didn't cover her own ears as well was because her arms were firmly pinned to the troll's side.

The trolls didn't seem bothered by the noise. They were looking at the humans with baffled expressions. "Grah?" said one uncertainly

Sings whimpered, and the troll holding him picked him up and cuddled him, saying worriedly, "Grah! Grah-grah-aaah?"

We have got to stop doing this, thought Nessilka wearily. *We know there's no conversation, we know there's nothing to understand, my head is going to come apart if I hear much more of this . . .*

"Graaaah?"

Finchbones crawled, inch by agonizing inch, toward the girl. He was still clutching the crossbow, perhaps planning to bludgeon her to death if nothing else presented itself.

John, closest to the source, had gone to his knees. He reached for his sister, but she stepped out of the way. Her eyes narrowed, and the voice, if anything, got worse. Nessilka felt as if a mule were kicking her repeatedly between the eyes.

Our brains are gonna melt. There's going to be blood coming out of our ears soon. It wasn't just trampling—those people died *of this.*

"Grawww . . ." said her troll. It fidgeted, crushing her more tightly against its side.

Nessilka's vision filmed with red mist.

Something moved.

It strode past the fire, past the torches, and even through the film of red, Nessilka thought it moved like a goblin.

. . . Blanchett?

Blanchett was wearing his helmet. He took one more step forward, reached up, and plucked the bear from his helm.

The voice redoubled. The girl had seen him. It focused, concentrated, and Nessilka began screaming because it drowned the sound out just a little, and that was good, and anyway, everybody else was screaming, too.

Blanchett wound up, took two running strides, and flung the bear across the sea of screaming elves.

It hit the girl square in the face.

Blanchett always did have good aim.

The voice ended in a very unmagical squawk. Nessilka considered how long the bear had been in battle—*months*—and how often it had been washed—*never*—and just how foul it must be.

Probably got a lot of Blanchett's rancid hair gel on there, too. I don't even want to know what that stuff's made of.

Even somebody who'd been surrounded by corpses for a week might draw the line at taking that particular bear to the face.

Sings-to-Trees yelled in Elvish.

The troll holding Nessilka dropped her, gently, and lumbered forward. The girl's face vanished under a large hooved paw.

"Graw?" it said.

Sings-to-Trees nodded.

John stood up. "I'm sorry, sir," he said, to no one in particular. "I have to take her away. It's too dangerous. I'll make a hole."

Finchbones coughed, spat, and tried to say something. His vocabulary did not seem to be up to either "summary execution" or "extradition," but John nodded gravely. "I'm sorry, sir," he said again. "Doing this is bad?—I think? Against orders?"

"Yes," said Finchbones.

John nodded again. "Yes. But it'll be . . . worse. Much worse. She's dangerous. I shouldn't have left her alone. She just . . . wasn't this strong before." He nodded several times, as if cementing this idea firmly in his head. "I'll have to take her away, sir."

"Where will you go?" asked Sings.

"Somewhere—far. Remote?" John glanced at Sings, then away. "I go there sometimes? It's safe. There's nobody there."

"That's probably good," said Sings.

"Yes, sir."

John paused, closed one eye, and spat blue light. Nessilka cringed in memory of what that blue light could do.

Finchbones cursed and dropped his crossbow, shaking his fingers. Blue light slithered over the weapon.

"Very sorry, sir. But she's my *sister*."

Finchbones said something grim in Elvish to Sings.

Nessilka recognized an order when she heard it. Sings said something right back. She didn't recognize that, but by the tone, Sings wasn't particularly concerned about following orders.

He's a civilian, Finchbones, you can't court-martial him . . . much as you might want to . . .

John reached up and grabbed the air, as he had once before on the battlefield. Nessilka's stomach lurched again as he pulled downward, and the air showed . . . somewhere else.

It was daylight there. It looked like an alpine meadow. Mountains rose up toward a blue bowl of sky.

"Excuse me, sir?" said John to the troll.

"Graw?"

"Let her go," said Sings, "and Matthien, you will *not* shoot one of my trolls, or I will raise hell clear to the Great Glade."

Finchbones looked as if he'd eaten something extremely sour.

The troll handed her to John. She gulped a breath, and her brother promptly put a hand over her mouth. "Only until we go through," he told her. "Then you can do whatever you like."

He stepped through the hole in the air.

It hung there for a second longer—long enough to see John release his sister and for her to gaze around with wide eyes—and then the hole closed up, and the fabric of the world healed itself.

A silence fell. It did not break until Finchbones let out a long, disgusted sigh and picked up his no-longer-glowing crossbow.

Sings reached down, dusted off the bear, and handed it back to Blanchett.

"And now," he said, "I think we've all got a lot of talking to do."

Three days later, Nessilka sat in Sings-to-Trees's kitchen and peeled potatoes.

Captain Finchbones, much-decorated leader of elite elven rangers, sat next to her and peeled them as well. Sings seemed to feel it would be good for him.

Finchbones could detach the entire peel in one continuous sweep of the knife, which was very impressive, but Nessilka's rather cruder technique produced three peeled potatoes for every one of his.

There was probably some kind of deep philosophical point there, but Nessilka wasn't inclined to go digging for it.

It was pretty much all over now. The goblins would leave tomorrow for Goblinhome and would be provided a ranger escort the entire way. Meanwhile, Finchbones and a small group of his men had been staying with Sings. They pretended they weren't there as guards, and Nessilka pretended her goblins weren't being guarded, and everyone was reasonably happy.

Thumper had made a full recovery. So had Blanchett. The bear not only had a set of stripes sewn on his arm, it was possibly the first teddy bear in history to have received a medal for service to the elven nation.

Nessilka and Murray had them as well. They were delicate silver leafy things—about what you'd expect from eleven medals. She didn't know how long they'd last in combat, but it had been a nice gesture.

And . . . maybe more than a gesture. She glanced over at Finchbones.

He smiled. "Thinking?"

"Wondering if this is really going to change anything."

Finchbones nodded slowly. His command of the human language had improved somewhat from use, but it still took him a minute to think through a complicated sentence. (Sings-to-Trees had read him the riot act about not speaking the language of people under his protection, and Finchbones, to his credit, was trying. She suspected that his opinion of her had increased radically when she proved more eloquent than he was.)

"Maybe change," he said finally. "Don't know why anything changes. Maybe small thing."

Nessilka tossed another potato on the pile.

"I think things will change," said Sings. "It's a good story. People latch onto stories." He frowned into the soup he was making. "We've got to do something, anyway—can you imagine putting that poor soul in the army?"

Finchbones and Nessilka exchanged glances.

Might be the best place for him, really, Nessilka thought, *if your description's right. He needed structure and someone to tell him what to do when. Pity they didn't get his sister, too, or those people might still be alive.*

But you couldn't say that sort of thing to Sings-to-Trees. There was something very . . . *civilian* . . . about Sings. Nessilka concentrated on her potatoes.

From what they'd been able to piece together—from the old man, and from what Sings had learned from the wizard in the few hours they'd spent together—a picture had emerged. John and Lisabet had indeed been orphans in the village of Elliot's Cross, until the army had come to recruit John.

Contrary to Lisabet's complaints, he had gone willingly.

Not like you could draft someone who can simply walk out through a hole in the air . . .

Lisabet's talent had been judged both too weak to recruit—which meant that either someone had been incredibly shortsighted, or she had been too cunning to let anyone know the extent of her abilities, or her powers had increased dramatically. There were all kinds of reasons *that* could happen, from puberty to stress, and there was just no telling.

Frankly, they might have thought that dragging everybody toward you, friend or foe, was more trouble than it was worth . . .

Now they were on shakier ground, conjecture-wise, but apparently Lisabet had not taken kindly to the people who were taking care of her, and she refused to believe that her brother would go off without her. She had presumably decided that the problem was the village, and if everybody in the village was gone, they would have to bring John back to take care of her.

It was the sort of plan a child would come up with—simple, self-centered, and utterly heartless.

And there were more than forty dead humans and a great many dead animals as a result.

Nessilka pitched another potato in the pile.

The rest, of course, was fate. When the Nineteenth had charged the wizard, he had panicked and tried to flee home out of pure instinct. Possibly if they hadn't all piled through, he might have made it back to Elliot's Cross, but the shock had been too much and he dropped them only partway to the goal.

We're probably all lucky we didn't just vanish in some weird blue space between worlds.

Finchbones was livid knowing that there was a rogue wizard on the loose, but they had no leads at all for where the pair might have gone. Nessilka was of the opinion that they had gone very far away indeed. Something about the view through the hole had seemed . . . remote. Hopefully John could control his sister. Despite having faced him over a battlefield, Nessilka wished him well.

Someone yanked the door open, and eight goblins piled

into Sings-to-Trees's kitchen. Two elves followed, slightly more decorously . . . or as decorous as anyone can look with an armful of zucchini.

"Sarge!"

"Sarge!"

"Sarge, the bear says—"

"Sarge, I get to take Wiggles back to Goblinhome, right?"

"I've been checking our maps, Sarge, against the elven ones, and our route takes us past a couple of human villages—"

"Sarge, Mishkin hit me!"

"Mushkin hit me first, Sarge!"

"I can't leave Wiggles, Sarge! He'll pine!"

"—and I was hoping we might be able to purchase a couple of lenses for the looky-tube-thing—"

"He took my zucchini!"

"It was my zucchini first!"

Nessilka put her hand over her eyes. Finchbones grinned down at the potatoes. Weasel hooked her finger into the raccoon's cage and stroked the top of its head.

She dealt with things in order of importance. "Wiggles goes with us. No kitten left behind. Murray, we'll see how it goes. Blanchett, have the bear prepare a full report after dinner. Mishkin, Mushkin, I don't care who started it, it's *my* zucchini now, and you will both be washing dishes after dinner!"

She drew a deep breath and delivered the final and inevitable coda.

"Gloober, get your finger out of there!"

"Awww . . ."

Well, at least things were getting back to normal. And maybe nothing would change, and the war would still go on, and they'd be right back to gruel and marching up hillsides in the dark.

Maybe Finchbones was right, and you never knew why anything changed. Maybe it was all down to small things.

Like teddy bears. And kittens.

And goblins.

AUTHOR'S NOTE

Nine Goblins was the first book I ever self-published, and will forever have a soft spot in my heart as a result. It was 2013 and I was writing children's books for a living under my real name, and I had run headlong into the great problem of writing children's books, which is that you are not allowed to write certain things. Arson, murder, and stacking bodies like cordwood are frowned upon. (Yes, I did point out that kids would love these things. My editor pointed out that parents and grandparents buy the books. She wasn't wrong, though I still think the occasional grisly murder is nothing a well-adjusted child can't cope with.)

I often say that inside every children's author is a frustrated horror author. It's not an exaggeration to say that T. Kingfisher was that horror author. I was (and still am) incredibly proud of the children's books I wrote, but dammit, sometimes the logical thing to do is just burn the haunted house down and walk away, preferably in slow motion, while backlit by flames.

So I wrote Nine Goblins, based on my love of Pratchett and James Herriot (Sings-to-Trees is a direct descendant of having read *All Creatures Great and Small* about fifty times at a formative age) and then discovered that no one had any idea how to sell a weird goofy novella by a children's author, particularly a novella with such a high body count.

It was 2013, self-publishing was still a brave new frontier.

I picked a pen name and put the book online. The initial version had infinite typos and chapter three appeared twice. My advertising consisted of posting on Twitter and LiveJournal. My initial cover was rejected by Amazon because it had goblin nipples. If it was possible to do something wrong, I found a way.

Somehow, it worked. Don't ask me how. *Nine Goblins* was never a runaway bestseller, despite *two whole Livejournal posts*, but year in and year out, it kept buying me groceries. It almost felt as if the goblins were taking care of me. Moreover, it was proof of concept. I could write a book for adults. Suddenly I had something to do with various stories floating around that were definitely not children's books.

So I wrote another one. And another one. Nobody stopped me. Eventually T. Kingfisher was getting bigger royalty checks than Ursula Vernon, and T. was allowed to swear in interviews. And then actual brick-and-mortar publishers got involved, who had staff that would catch things like duplicate chapter threes, and who were presumably willing to airbrush out goblin nipples, should the need arise, which streamlined things enormously.

I've written a lot of books as T. Kingfisher now. None of them would have happened without the goblins of the Whinin' Nineteenth, and I am so delighted to have them get out to a wider audience.

Of course, these things would also not have happened without my very supportive agent Helen, who said "Sure, give this self-pub thing a try, just yell when you need to sell audio and foreign rights."

You wouldn't be reading this snazzy updated version right now if not for my editor Lindsey Hall and the gang at Tor Books, who have brought back the novella in a big way, and who thought more people needed to meet the goblins.

As always, huge thanks to my husband Kevin. I created Sings-to-Trees before we met—and I have the documentation to prove it—but people could be forgiven for thinking otherwise.

And finally, thank you to everyone who has been a friend of the goblins since the beginning and to everyone who is discovering them for the first time. It's been a long strange road, and somewhere along it is a goblin complaining that their feet hurt.

T. Kingfisher
Edgewood, New Mexico
2025

ABOUT THE AUTHOR

T. KINGFISHER writes fantasy, horror, and occasional oddities, including *Nettle & Bone, Thornhedge, A Sorceress Comes to Call, What Moves the Dead,* and *A House With Good Bones.* Under a pen name, she also writes bestselling children's books. She lives in New Mexico with her dog, cats, and husband who is a dead ringer for Sings-to-Trees.

For more fantastic fiction, author events,
exclusive excerpts, competitions, limited editions and more

VISIT OUR WEBSITE
titanbooks.com

LIKE US ON FACEBOOK
facebook.com/titanbooks

FOLLOW US ON TWITTER AND INSTAGRAM
@TitanBooks

EMAIL US
readerfeedback@titanemail.com